the Sonshine Sister club

Woes of a Really, Very Bad Haircut

ISBN: 9798987423646

Library of Congress Control Number: 2023920976

Printed in the United States of America

the Sonshine Sister club

Woes of a Really, Very Bad Haircut

By Shelbey Kendall

To all the girls who have thought

a bad haircut is the end of the world.

Dear Jesus,

My mom bought me a new hairbrush last week. I know You know, but I wanted to tell You myself. She says it's important that there are no ~~nots~~ knots in my hair. I don't think it matters. I told her hats are fine. So, she bought a de...tangle...ing spray. I told her that Jesus doesn't care about my hair. But she made me go see Mrs. Lucy at the salon. She chopped most of it off. Now it's too short to put in a ponytail. (Also, why is it called a ponytail?) I'm not happy about it. If You could please let my hair grow quickly, and with no knots, that would be great...Thanks.

Your Sonshine Sister,

Andie

Chapter 1

A New School Year

My name is Andie, or at least that's what my friends and family call me. My full name is Miranda Hope Wilson. I'm ten-years-old and I hate it. It's a horrible age to be. Everyone treats me like a child, and yet expects me to be a grown-up at times. *"Temper tantrums are for babies,"* they say, and yet, I watch adults throw temper tantrums all the time. It's so confusing.

I have two older brothers, Levi and Colton. They are pretty cool, except for the times they aren't. Those times they are extremely annoying. Levi is into soccer. I personally don't understand sports, but supposedly Levi is really good. Colton is the oldest. He's in high school, and well, he's also not interested in sports. He's interested in girls. It's embarrassing.

I should also mention we are homeschooled, so I spend a lot of time with my brothers. Even though we are different, and we sometimes get on each other's nerves, we would stand up for each other any day of the week.

I live in a small town, but not so small of a town that it only has dirt roads. We have pavement, a grocery store, a coffee shop, several restaurants including my favorite that serves Chinese food, and a handful of churches. My parents just started letting me ride my bicycle around town, but only sometimes, and only if I'm with my brothers or my friends.

My friends and I started a club a couple of years ago. There are five of us girls. We've all lived on the same street, Cherry Lane, for as long as we can remember. Even though we don't always like each other, we are still friends by proximity and now, the bond of our club. We are all different but we're also similar with our biggest similarity being our faith. We all love Jesus and that's what our club was founded on.

The Sonshine Sister Club, to be exact. We attend different churches, besides Sam and me. We attend the Lutheran Church. But our faith isn't about sharing the same church. We care about each other's hearts, and we all strive to become more like Jesus. We mess up a lot. Sometimes I feel like I mess up the most. However, we meet once a week to talk about the good we see Jesus doing in our lives and sometimes even the ways we don't see Him working.

Today is our last meeting before the new school year starts, even though we'll still meet on Saturday evenings when school begins. The members are Sam, Emma, Caroline, Sarah, and me, Andie.

Sam, short for Samantha, is my church friend and she goes to private school. She personally loves the plaid uniforms she must wear. She also loves brownies, especially if they are covered in sprinkles and whipped cream. Her favorite color is teal and she's very specific that it is teal, not turquoise.

Emma is also homeschooled. We go to the same homeschool co-op every Monday and often get together during the day once we've finished up our schoolwork. Her house is only two down from mine. She has an adorable puppy named Gus and she hates all things with chocolate chips. It's weird. I mean, who doesn't love chocolate chips?

Caroline attends Newport Elementary School, except this year she's going to Middle School. She does ballet and almost always has her black hair swooped up into a neat and tidy bun. She says her mom brushes her hair morning and night to ensure there are no tangles. I can't imagine. It sounds like a horror movie. Not that I know anything about horror movies. I've never seen one.

Sarah attends public school with Caroline and is also starting Middle School this year. She always seems to be nervous about everything. She nibbles on her nails often and chews through a package of bubblegum each day. She loves science, which I find odd because science is my least favorite subject. But I often ask her questions when I get stuck on my own schoolwork because science is also my mom's least favorite subject. She asks me to Google answers a lot. She calls it scientific research.

And then there's me, Andie. I love my friends even if I think they are strange at times.

We meet in my bedroom which means I unfortunately must keep it clean. This makes my parents extremely grateful for The Sonshine Sister

Club. Today I tidied it up but even with the tidying, my bookshelves are currently overflowing with more knick-knacks than books (knick-knacks is a fun word for *small, decorative items*), and my baskets are brimming with enough crafts to last a normal person ten years. But I'm a crafting expert and I estimate there are about four months of materials in those baskets.

There's a soft knock at my door.

"Andie, the girls are all here," my mom announces. I love my mother. She smells like brown sugar and patchouli. I know most ten-year-olds probably don't know what patchouli is, but my mom loves essential oils. It's a plant with weird looking flowers that bloom from it, but it smells earthy and like my mom.

"I'm ready," I reply, giving a last glance over my room. Everything seems okay, and honestly, if my mom brings us a snack, I don't think anyone will notice if there are a few things, or a lot of things, stuffed underneath my bed.

It isn't long and I hear the girls shuffling down the hallway, their giggling entering my room before they do.

"Andie! Your hair!" Sarah squeals.

She wraps me up in a hug that feels awkward and yet, normal. I also notice shiny braces adorning her teeth as she smiles. So much for that bubblegum chewing.

"My hair, but what about your teeth?! Braces?!" I exclaim, diverting the conversation from the unfortunate haircut. I didn't want to talk about the short bob that itched against my cheeks.

Sarah's shoulders slump. "The orthodontist says I may have them for a while. They are absolutely awful. My mouth throbbed for days. My dad told me I'd have several appointments to tighten them. It's like a prison in my mouth."

I run my tongue over my own teeth, silently sending a prayer up to God that He makes them perfectly straight. "That's awful, Sarah! I am so sorry!"

I watch as my friends all sit on the floor, making our usual circle. I take a seat, butterfly style, letting my legs flop up and down. Then I notice crumbs tangled in my carpet threads and I attempt to pick them out before everyone else notices.

Sam takes her teal, glittered notebook out of her tote bag adorned with pins of cats and coffee cups. Her mother owns the coffee shop and she's already addicted to the taste of espresso. She's the notetaker at the meetings, writing down our prayer requests and putting a heart beside any prayer that was answered from weeks before.

"I can't believe summer is over," Caroline mutters, a slight disdain in her voice. Disdain can mean a variety of things but in this instance, I knew it meant she was *not looking forward to school starting up again*, and I figured it was because she was entering Middle School.

"You get to start school in a new building!" I shout a little too enthusiastically, and even I realize the words were forced.

Caroline rolls her eyes at me before her chin drops to her chest. "You can try to list all the exciting things about Middle School, but I've heard them all, Andie. Middle School is full of awkward kids trying to figure out who they are before they go to high school."

"I'm excited," Sarah adds, even though her nervous chewing of her fingernails tells a different story.

"It'll be so much fun," Emma interjects, trying to add some encouragement.

"But we are the young ones, again," Caroline whines. "Fifth graders are like Kindergarteners in Middle School."

I shrug my shoulders, not having anything of value to add to the conversation. I wouldn't know what it felt like to enter a new building with new teachers and new schedules. Half the time, I did my schoolwork in my pajamas sprawled out across my unmade bed.

"Well, I'm ready for school to start next Monday," Sam beams. "My mom pressed my new plaid skirt and vest last night. I love getting to wear my uniform."

I look over Sam's current clothing choice of jean shorts and a white T-shirt, just now realizing how plain she dressed even outside of her school uniform.

She did like her accessories though, if they sparkled, or were teal.

"What about you, Andie?" Caroline asks. "When do you start school?"

"Well, I mean, we kind of school all year long," I mumble, always confused about how to answer this question. "But mom says I'm officially in fifth grade in two weeks."

"Emma?" Sarah asks.

"Not until September," she replies. "My dad just got back, so we are spending as much time with him while he is here."

Emma's dad is in the military. I think he's pretty high up in rank, but I don't know for sure. I really couldn't tell you what ranks there are. I just know he keeps people safe, including my family. Military men and women are brave heroes, but I don't know how Emma, her mom, and her sisters do it. It must be extremely hard for him to be gone for such long periods of time.

We all smile and nod, never sure how to relate to what Emma goes through.

"Shall we?" Sam asks brightly, holding the glittery, teal notebook up for all to see. "First, answered prayers. Anyone have any of those?"

Sam opens the notebook, using her pen with the furry, teal pom as a guide to sort through her scribblings. I watch as she bites her lower lip, concentrating on the things we've previously had her write down.

"How's Gus, Emma?" Sam finally asks, breaking the silence of no one offering to go first.

"Oh yes!" Emma exclaims. "Gus is great. The fleas are gone, thank goodness. I unfortunately found a few on myself. Mom made me take a flea bath. It was mortifying. But the fleas are gone. On Gus and me."

I watch Sam draw a heart beside the prayer request.

"Anyone else?" Sam asks.

Caroline leans over to peer at the notebook in Sam's lap. "You can just scratch out my prayer request from last week."

Sam's head quickly turns towards Caroline, her blonde curls whipping around her face. "Was it answered?"

"No. I don't like him anymore," Caroline mutters with disgust.

Sarah leans over to me, whispering in my ear, "Brady asked another girl out."

Caroline glares at Sarah. "He's not my type anyway."

"Are we even old enough to have a type?" I ask with a tone that is slightly annoyed that this is part of our prayer requests. Caroline has always been boy crazy. I don't understand the obsession. Sure, some are cute but as a species, they are just plain weird. I'm perfectly fine to not worry about them for a few more years.

"Yes, we are old enough for a type, Andie," Caroline grumbles while she intentionally does an intense eye roll to show her irritation with me.

I ignore her frustration knowing she'll get over it soon enough and instead ask, "Any other answered prayers?"

Everyone is silent.

"New prayer requests then?" Sam questions, readying her pen to write.

"For my braces to not last forever," Sarah moans.

"For my sister to quit stealing my favorite socks," Emma adds.

"For Middle School to be the best experience I've ever had in my entire life," Caroline exaggerates.

"For perfect attendance this year," Sam says as she smiles at the notebook, her pen moving quickly. "Andie?"

"For my hair to grow back, and quickly," I say, finally acknowledging the haircut to my friends. I look around at everyone and catch Caroline smirking at me. I glare back.

"I actually love it," Emma compliments. "It's very you."

"I do, too," Sam says through a polite grin.

Sarah reaches over and rubs my back as if she is offering her condolences.

I blow the short, fuzzy strands out of my face before we all bow our heads to pray over everything we've just requested. I listen while Sam details the prayer out loud, but silently and quickly I say an extra prayer for my hair before Sam says, "Amen."

Dear Jesus,

I'm sorry. I really hate to request this again, but I haven't noticed Your healing touch ~~effecting~~ affecting my hair. Youth group started this week. I saw kids whispering and feared they were talking about me. My mom bought some colorful headbands thinking they'd help me love the haircut more. It didn't work. Please help a girl out.

Your Sonshine Sister,

Andie

Chapter 2

Fifth Grade and an Unfunny Brother

I'm officially in fifth grade, although it doesn't feel like too much has changed. Math is different this year. My mom switched my curriculum. I like it and it gives me hope that maybe one day I'll appreciate science more. I mean, miracles can happen, right?

The Sonshine Sister Club has met twice since school started for Caroline, Sarah, and Sam. Emma hasn't started yet and everyone called her lucky, but I really know she doesn't feel lucky. Her dad leaves again in just a few weeks.

Caroline has a new crush. He's a seventh grader. Matthew is supposedly gorgeous, but I have yet to meet a gorgeous seventh-grade boy. My brother is a seventh-grade boy. I definitely wouldn't call him gorgeous. His current plight, which I learned this week during my vocabulary lesson, means *unfortunate situation*, are the pimples that are sprinkled across his nose and cheeks like inflamed, red freckles. I sure hope Jesus spares me when it comes to acne.

Sam's prayer request for perfect attendance had to be scratched off last week. She caught an end-of-summer cold. She was devastated. My mom sent me over to her house with homemade chicken noodle soup and a roller bottle of essential oils that smelled like cinnamon. It didn't revive her quickly enough, though. She was marked absent, and I'm pretty sure the disappointment in missing school made her more unwell than the cold itself.

Sarah announced she was going to join a volleyball team. I asked her what would happen if a volleyball hit her in the face with her braces. She winced and then put it on our prayer request list to protect her from shanked hits and spikes to the mouth. A worthy request, I believed. Much more worthy than Caroline's request to make Matthew notice her.

Emma has only asked for her dad to be kept safe for his upcoming deployment. Deployment means *the movement of military troops or equipment to a place or position for action*. Both times she's asked for this prayer request, it has made me feel silly requesting that my hair gain some kind of supernatural growing power. But Pastor Will preached a sermon on Sunday about asking God for help in everything, the big and the small. So, I know it's okay to talk about the smallest and silliest things to God, but I really do want Emma's dad to be kept safe more than I want my hair to grow back out. Although, I really hope my hair will grow out sooner than later. I think it's okay to ask for both.

My mom is currently upstairs in her studio working on a commissioned piece. She's an artist in the afternoons while my brothers and I work on our assignments from what she taught us in the morning. I can hear the hum of her speaker playing loud music. It's so loud it vibrates my bedroom ceiling.

I'm currently working on my handwriting. Mom tells me all the time about the importance of knowing how to write and read cursive. She calls it a lost art to all the electronic devices kids use these days. I suppose it may be true, but I also really love to type. It makes me feel important, like I'm penning the next bestselling novel.

I don't know what I want to be when I grow up yet. I've thought about becoming an author, or maybe an artist like my mom, or maybe a chef. I really love to cook. Tuesdays are my night in the kitchen. I get to fix whatever I want for family dinner but then I also must clean up. Even with the dirty dishes, it's one of my favorite nights.

But for now, I'm just a fifth grader. My dad reminds me all the time that I have the rest of my life to figure things out, but that really doesn't make sense. At some point you have to figure things out. I think it's just something adults say to try to make you enjoy your childhood more. My dad often says, *"Trust me, you'll miss being a kid someday."* So, maybe they just know something I don't know yet.

My door bursts open and Levi jumps onto my bed making all my books go bouncing off.

"Levi!" I scream. I begin to grind my teeth. I want to call him something unkind but our devotion this morning was over the importance of our words. *"Your words are tools, children. You can either build wonderful things or destroy everything with what you say,"* mom had said.

And I know it's true. The Bible says the power of life and death exists in our tongue, which is kind of a strange concept if I'm honest. I get what God meant by it but sometimes when I read the verse, I imagine my tongue becoming some kind of snake, like a boa constrictor, that leaps out of my mouth and strangles my brother.

In fact, that's what I'm thinking about right now, but instead I bite down on my tongue before I say something I might regret. Or if not regret, at least get in trouble for when he tells my mom or dad about it.

"What's up, Andie?" Levi says casually as he lays down on my bed getting his gross germs all over my bedsheets that are covered in purple flowers and butterflies.

"I was working on my handwriting," I say, trying to not sound angry. "Can you please get off my bed?"

"I think your mattress is better than mine," Levi replies, wiggling his body deeper within my sheets, wrinkling them as he does. "I'm pretty sure as the baby you get the best and newest things."

I roll my eyes at him. "I'm not a baby."

"Well, technically, you are the baby, Andie. You are the youngest," he teases, and I can feel the color in my cheeks go from a happy pink to an enraged red.

I construct a prayer in my head to help me not call my brother mean names while I take a deep breath. Instead of answering him, I quickly pick up the books that are sprawled out on my floor, stacking them in my arms. Mom always tells me to ignore him when he gets into his playful moods, but there is nothing playful about it to me. Playful would mean I was having fun. I am not having fun.

He continues to smirk at me from my bed, his hands cradling his head of greasy, brown hair. "I think I'll just take a nap here," he dares to say.

"Can you please leave so I can finish my schoolwork? Emma is going to be here soon," I request through a forced, polite smile. I'm going to have to wash my sheets.

"You aren't finished with your school yet? I've been done for hours," he mutters as he stretches and yawns, still refusing to move from my bed.

I feel the slither of my tongue wanting to turn to a snake, but inside my head I hear my mom's voice reminding us to use our words wisely. I silently go through the fruits of the spirits in my head. Love. Joy. Peace. Patience. Kindness. Goodness. Faithfulness. Gentleness. Self-control. I currently feel none of these things.

I place my books on my desk, which is more often used for crafting than schoolwork. I turn around, crossing my arms as I look at my annoying brother. "I'm serious, Levi. Please leave."

"Take a joke, Andie. I thought maybe that new haircut of yours would lighten you up. Get it? Less hair, so it made you feel lighter?" Levi laughs at his joke that makes my brain stop repeating the fruits of the spirit and instead release all the words I want to say to him. How dare he mention my haircut. He knows I hate it.

"You're such a jerk, Levi! I asked you to leave. GET OUT OF MY ROOM! NOW!" I yell as I march towards him with my fist curled up beside me quivering. I hope I have enough strength to leave a bruise when my punch meets his arm. Then I hear my mom's music abruptly shut off.

"What is going on down there?!" she yells. There is a prickly irritation to her muffled words that come from my ceiling. I never know how she does it. How she can hear everything. It's like she's bugged our rooms. That's *when people hide secret microphones or cameras to spy on others*. I saw it in a movie once. But she's told us the only thing possibly spying on us in our room is our Alexa. Which I kind of believe. Every once in a while, Alexa spouts off information I never asked for. I even made my friends whisper during The Sonshine Sister Club once thinking Alexa was listening.

Levi smirks. I wiggle my fingers loose from my fist and then I say, "Please, get out."

He does so, finally.

I hear my mom's footsteps on the creaky staircase and soon she's knocking on my open bedroom door. "Everything okay down here, Andie?"

I take a deep breath through my nose before tattling on my brother. "Levi came in and wouldn't leave. I asked him many times and he just laid there, on my bed, dirtying my sheets with his grossness.

Then he called me a baby. Well, the baby of the family, and made fun of my hair."

"Levi!" my mom yells as she walks into my room. "Get in here, please!"

Levi peeks his head around the corner. "I was just told to get out."

"Did you make fun of Andie's hair?" she asks calmly, but I can hear the simmer in her tone. My mom sometimes boils over like an unwatched pot of noodles. One minute, they are boiling just fine. A perfect bubble. And then the next minute, you have to do a deep cleaning of the stove after the water spills over and sizzles on the burner making a real mess.

"Not exactly," my brother says sweetly as he looks at our mom with his big, blue, puppy-dog eyes.

"So, what did you say?" she asks, placing her hands on her hips. It's never good when moms place their hands on their hips.

"I just told her that I thought having less hair would make her lighten up. Take a joke...you know. She never gets my jokes," he explains.

"Okay," she pauses to take a breath. "You know she doesn't like her haircut, so it was unnecessary to say anything about it. Secondly, your jokes aren't always funny, Levi. We've talked about this. Sometimes it sounds funny in our head, but it isn't funny when it comes out of our mouth."

This isn't the first time she's addressed Levi's sense of humor. He always thinks he's super funny. I personally think he'd make an awful comedian.

"But it's still funny in my head," Levi says, leaning up against the doorframe with his arms crossed. His blue eyes sparkled with mischief. Mischief means *playful misbehavior or troublemaking.* Levi was always getting into mischief, and it was the troublemaking kind.

"Then let me put it this way," my mother begins. "When it is in your head, ask yourself if you think your sister will think it's funny. If you don't believe she will, keep it to yourself."

"Fine," Levi mutters.

My mother raises her eyebrows and we both know what that means.

"I'm sorry, Andie," Levi grumbles, not even looking at me.

My mother clears her throat.

This time he steps over to me and wraps me up in a smelly hug. My face is squished into his armpit that strangely smells like Cheetos and B.O. That's the *acronym for body odor*. Then he says again, "I'm sorry, Andie."

My mother may have thought the apology was more genuine, but my nostrils had officially been attacked.

Dear Jesus,

I am still incredibly unhappy with my hair, but more than that my brother needs help. He stinks. Really bad. I'm afraid no girl will ever like him. Not that I want them to. Please, PLEASE never let Caroline think he is cute. So, maybe always keep him gross.

And thanks for the eighth of an inch of hair growth. Can we please double that soon? Triple? Quadruple?

Your Sonshine Sister,

Andie

Chapter 3

A Sorry Saturday Night

The headband scratches at my scalp and pinches behind my ears like some kind of lobster claw attempting to make my head separate from my body. I furiously grab the pincher made of plastic and purple satin and remove it from my short, ginger wisps. Did I mention I'm a redhead? It's not really red like Ariel from *The Little Mermaid*. I personally think it's blonde, but my mom says I'm wrong. I've agreed with her, but I don't really agree with her.

"He's just dreamy." I hear Caroline's words swirl through the air reminding me that I'm supposed to be listening to everyone's prayer requests, but she's been going on and on for ten minutes about her first interaction with Matthew that happened this week. He smiled at her when she waved at him. That's it. A smile. And supposedly that smile means he's potential boyfriend material.

"Boys are weird," I mutter with irritation. I blame the headband for being so cranky with my words.

"You just don't like that boys like me and not you," Caroline spits. And literally, she does spit. I see the splatter of her saliva become molecules in my bedroom air. Disgusting.

"Supposedly they do," I whisper.

"Excuse me?!" Caroline shouts. "What is that supposed to mean?"

"He smiled at you, Caroline," I murmur, rolling my eyes. "It was one smile, and it was because you waved at him."

"Well, that's rude, Miranda Hope Wilson," Caroline replies, emphasizing every syllable of my name. She's been doing this to all of us in The Sonshine Sister Club lately. When she feels she's right and we're wrong, she calls us out by our full name as if the power our moms have in doing this is somehow granted to her. But that's not how full names work. It's just annoying when Caroline does it. It's scary when moms do.

"Is it rude?" I question, standing up from my bedroom floor. "Because I don't think listening to the way Matthew's dark hair flops perfectly to one side, or how his eyes sparkle when he is laughing with his buddies in the hall, or really anything about your current obsession with a boy needs to be scribbled down on our prayer list."

I look down at Caroline, my hands on my hips. She scrambles to stand, her hands now on her hips. We are facing off in an awkward battle. I feel the tension between us grow and sweat begins to soak through my favorite shirt. It's the one with fluttery sleeves that makes me feel like a princess butterfly. It's also blue, but not teal much to Sam's dismay.

"And your hair does?" she shouts with spit once again leaving her lips. "Do you think we care about how fast your hair is growing week after week? It's hair, Andie. If you would have done better and brushed it, you'd still have it."

I really dislike Caroline right now. My hair was not insignificant. It was something I had to deal with every single day. Of course, she wouldn't care. Her mother brushes hers. Mine wouldn't. She told me I was old enough to learn how to take care of my own hair. I sure proved her wrong.

Sam stands. "Stop it. Both of you. We are supposed to care about what one another cares about. That's how this works. It might not be something we think is awesome, or even a problem, but that's not the point. If it matters to one of us, it matters to all of us."

I feel heat rush to my cheeks, embarrassed at the temper tantrum I'd just displayed in front of all my friends. I sit back down. So does Caroline, but when she does so, she crosses her arms, and she doesn't say anything the rest of the meeting.

"I'm sorry," I mumble. There are nods and smiles from everyone in the circle besides Caroline.

Sarah reaches over and pats my knee. "We care about your hair, Andie."

But even though Sarah says the words, the ones Caroline had said sink deeper. Was it silly for me to ask continually for my hair to grow back? Did my friends think I was ridiculous for doing so? I was the one who created my own problem. My mom had tried to give me tools to help. She'd lectured me many times about properly shampooing and conditioning my hair. But I hadn't taken her advice. My hair had continued to tangle into so many knots that I couldn't stand the pain when I finally did try to brush it.

The rest of the meeting, I kept my lips zipped up. In my mind I even attached a lock to the zipper pull. A pretty lock, of course. One shaped like a silver heart dangling from my lips.

I heard the rest of the prayer requests. In addition to my hair and Caroline's crush, Emma once again asked for her dad's safety overseas. Sarah asked for her mouth to be numb when she had her first appointment to tighten her braces. Sam asked for God's favor to be voted in as class president at her school.

Sam prayed over it all and they all promptly left. They all gave good excuses to leave early. Most of the time we played a game or did a craft together but not this Saturday night. Emma said she was training Gus to sit and couldn't miss an evening of it. Caroline said she needed to practice a ballet routine for her lessons on Monday. Sarah said her family was having a movie night. Sam said she had homework. Which I didn't fully believe because Sam always has her homework done by Saturday night.

I'm sitting on my bed in my empty room when there is a soft knocking on my bedroom door.

"Can I come in, sweetie?" I hear my dad ask.

"Yes," I mumble. I watch the handle wiggle and then my dad enters my room. My dad works hard at something I don't understand. He's some kind of engineer. But he always makes time for his family. It's something I've always appreciated.

"The girls left early tonight," he states as he makes his way to sit on my bed beside me.

"They all said they had things to do," I reply, but I'm sure my dad can hear my own doubt in the words.

He nods his head and then puts his arm around my shoulders, pulling me to his side. He kisses the top of my head and all I can think about is how slow my hair is sprouting. "Well, I guess that gives me some extra time with you. What do you want to do?"

"Uno?" I suggest.

"A game of Uno sounds fun," he agrees.

We play a lot of games in our house. My brothers have been playing less since becoming older. They claim that games are for babies, but my parents love to play games. I know they just hate losing because I win almost every time.

I jump off my bed to retrieve the cards. I watch as my dad slides down to the floor, twisting his legs into a pretzel. My dad has long legs. It's something my older brother, Colton inherited. Colton is pleased with the development. My brother Levi and I take after my mom. She's short. Levi sulks a lot about it. Especially when Colton chooses to tower over him to taunt him.

I grab the cards and give half of the deck for my dad to shuffle. We shuffle quietly, handing each other half of our stack occasionally. One thing we've learned from many card games played is you can never shuffle too much to ensure fairness.

"So, what's bothering you, Andie?" he questions. He's still shuffling without looking at his cards. Adults like to show off sometimes. It only makes me want to win even more.

"Nothing," I lie.

"So that argument you had with Caroline was nothing?" He says it gently, but it still feels like he just jabbed a needle in my eye. It's the worst when your parents overhear you when the words you say are not your best ones.

"Did mom hear?" I ask.

He shakes his head. "No, I thought I'd come talk to you about it first."

I wrinkle my nose, wishing the following conversation wouldn't have to take place.

"So, you really don't like your hair?" he questions, reaching over to tug a tuft of it playfully.

"I feel like I look like a boy," I mumble.

"Those weird creatures you don't like?" he teases. "You know, us boys aren't so bad."

I roll my eyes. It's not the same thing. He's my dad and he showers daily.

"You don't look like a boy, Andie," my dad says, but I don't believe him. I've always had long hair before now. Well, not when I was a baby. I was bald then. But for the part of my existence in which I cared about my hair, it's always been long. Now it wasn't. I felt like something was wrong with me.

"I just like my hair better long," I groan while I pull at the ends where my braids used to be. "This doesn't feel like me."

He nods his head, dealing us each seven cards before he says, "You go first."

It's yellow. I play a reverse card, which means it is my turn, and then a 'draw two' card.

"You stinker," he laughs. He takes two off the pile.

"I'm not the stinker, dad. Levi is," I reply, proud of my joke.

"One day you'll love that brother of yours," he comments.

"It's not that I don't love him," I explain. "It's that I don't love the way he smells or teases me. Seventh-grade boys are the worst."

"Caroline doesn't think so," my dad says with a smile.

I roll my eyes again.

"Andie, don't get me wrong, I am very happy that you don't like boys right now. Thrilled, actually. But there will come a day when you think they are cute and you are going to want your friends to care about it, too. Sam was right. When you girls founded The Sonshine Sister Club you vowed to care about what one another cares about knowing you all just want to love Jesus more." My dad says the words with good intentions. I know that. So, I take into consideration what he says.

But I still can't imagine the day I will think a boy is cute.

Dear Jesus,

I'm sorry for what I said to Caroline. It was not loving. In fact, the fruits of the Spirit seemed as if they had gone rotten in me. I still don't think boys are worth praying about unless it is about them figuring out how to use a bar of soap. I'm probably wrong about that, ~~two~~ too. Why do they smell so much? It's Sunday. I'm reading Scripture today in front of everyone which means my hair will be on display for all to see. Please make it grow about six inches in the next two hours.

Your Sonshine Sister,

Andie

Chapter Four

If Saturday Was Sorry, Then Sunday Was Sorrier

I smooth my dress out while sitting in the church pew. I'd picked my favorite dress to wear. It's deep violet in color and the long sleeves are a fun, transparent-like material. It also drapes past my knees, which I appreciate because they always seem to be scuffed or bruised.

I resist the urge to pluck the headband from my head. It's velvet and matches my dress. You would think it would be soft due to the velvet, but you would be wrong. It's metal underneath and I can feel it squeezing my head like my brother, Levi, squeezes at his pimples.

Pastor Will clears his throat at the microphone. "Today, our Scripture reading will be done by Miranda Wilson. Miranda?"

I'm pretty sure my dress has suddenly shrunk three sizes and is choking me. I don't feel like I can breathe. This is the first time I've done a Scripture reading. Pastor Will caught me after church last week and asked if I'd love to volunteer. I felt like I couldn't say no. If I said no, wasn't I saying no to God, too?

Colton nudges me out of my nervous breakdown. I shake my head and stand on legs that feel wobbly, like they've suddenly become cooked spaghetti noodles.

As I walk up to the front, I feel like my soul has left my body and is watching me from the large fan that hangs above the sanctuary. I look up at the enormous, vaulted ceiling and imagine I'm sitting on one of the fan's blades, legs crossed, praying fervently that I don't stumble over my feet or my words.

At some point on my slow journey to the pulpit, my soul rejoins my body. The three stairs I must summit feel like three hundred stairs (Summit in this instance means *to climb to the very* top). Once I finally get to the pulpit, I find myself trying to flip through the wispy pages of the Bible, attempting to locate the Scripture I've been tasked to read out loud. I almost forget about my hair until I look up into the congregation and catch my mom motioning for me to adjust my headband. My fingers fumble as I try to fix it without a mirror. I'm positive I've just made it worse.

"Today's reading is from Matthew, chapter ten, verses twenty-six through thirty-one," I mumble into the microphone, hearing the whine and shriek of it as my words bounce within the speaker. My mouth suddenly feels like I've swallowed one thousand cotton balls. I cough.

The words blur in front of me. I should have practiced more or memorized it. If I had memorized it, I could just close my eyes and pretend everyone wasn't looking at me.

"So do not be afraid of them," I begin and then I stutter through most of the verse until I get to a few certain words that send me into an emotional fury. "Even the very hairs of your head are all numbered."

I pause. I know I need to finish but the verses are talking about how there was no need to be afraid because God cares about each one of us more than he cares for the sparrows in the sky. But my hair. He knows how many hairs are on my head. Those frizzy, short strands. Why can He not make them grow faster? If He cares, wouldn't He care that I hate my hair?

A haughty huff of air escapes my lips and echoes in the microphone, vibrating within the sanctuary. I watch as a few people in the front row wince.

My face turns as red as a Red Delicious apple, or that horrible red swimsuit my mom bought me that made me look like I was one of the lifeguards at the pool. Redder than my hair that is not red, but blonde. Not that there is much of it to really tell.

"So don't be afraid. You are worth more than many sparrows," I quickly mumble before shutting the Bible and practically sprinting back to my seat beside my brother.

I hear Levi snicker but then I hear him grunt with pain as Colton digs his elbow into Levi's side. It was more discreet than slapping him upside the head, which is what Colton normally did at home. My mom was constantly telling them to keep their hands to themselves. Then Colton patted my knee to show support even though I knew he was supporting a fool. A fool that just got mad at God in front of the whole church.

I'm lost in my embarrassment for the rest of the service and find much relief when Pastor Will gives his final, "Amen".

Seconds later, Sam is hugging me. She knows about the woes of my haircut. Weeks of prayer requests with no hearts beside any of them in Sam's notebook meant I was still suffering from the unfortunate chopping. At least one of my Sonshine Sisters was here to understand. I lean into her but force myself not to cry.

"It's your first reading, Andie. I'm sure everyone just thought it was nerves," Sam whispered in my ear, and I know she could be right.

"Great job today, Miranda." Pastor Will interrupts Sam and me, extending his hand for a hearty handshake.

"Thanks, Pastor Will," I mumble, giving him my best polite smile even though I don't feel like smiling while shaking his hand.

"Samantha, would you like to do the Scripture reading next Sunday?" he asks, turning to face my friend.

"I would love to, Pastor Will! Can you text my mom the verses?" Sam smiles brightly at him. Sam has read the Scripture in church many times. She's great at getting up in front of people and dazzling them with her charm. She doesn't even stutter over her words. When she reads it sounds soothing, not like when I read today, and it sounded like a barking seal that was choking on a fish.

"Sounds good," Pastor Will replies to Sam. "You two have a beautiful Sunday. May God bless you both."

But Pastor Will has no idea how undeserving I am of a blessing right now. Sam deserves to have both of our blessings.

"Ready?" my dad asks, and I am most definitely ready to leave church. I sure hope Pastor Will never asks me to read Scripture again.

I nod my head and give Sam one last hug. "Elections this week, right?"

"Yes," she replies with a dance of nerves in her response.

"Good luck," I say. "You will make a wonderful President."

I mean it, too, even though I couldn't give her a smile. She really would make a great President. She's always timely, cares about others, and is great about making sure things get done. It's why she's in charge of the prayer notebook at The Sonshine Sister Club meetings.

Sam smiles at me before I turn to leave with my family. Levi attempts to trip me as we exit out the large, wooden double doors. I glare at him, kicking him in the shin instead.

Our mom steps between us. "Seriously, at church?"

Mom gives dad a look that means he needs to intervene. He steps over and loops his arm through mine, escorting me the rest of the way to the van. I would feel regret, but I've already given up on the day. I'm mad about my hair, mad that God won't fix it, embarrassed about getting mad in front of everyone at church, and annoyed that I have a brother that seems to exist only to torment me. My mom has said that sometimes we don't get to choose our circumstances, but we do get to choose how we react to them. I'm choosing to react poorly. I know that. But I really don't want to act any other way.

I sit in the third row of our van on the bench seat, crossing my arms. I feel my lips scrunch into a pout. I watch as my parents whisper words to each other in the front, most likely trying to decide how to deal with me later. I glance down at my shoes. They are a pair of scuffed, ankle boots that are at least one size too small for my feet. My mom promised we'd look at the thrift store for a new pair, but for now it feels like I have clown feet stuffed into a pair of shoes made for a doll.

The boys are talking about something soccer related. Even Colton is attempting to act like he cares about what Levi cares about. It seems I'm the only one who is struggling to care about anything other than myself.

We pull into the Chinese restaurant. It's our Sunday tradition. At least something is good about today.

We pile out of the van and enter the familiar smell of sweet and sour sauce and Lo Mein noodles. I think I feel a slight stirring of happiness, but it only lasts a few minutes. When I go through the buffet, I notice they are out of egg rolls. My favorite. My dad asks our waitress if there are more coming, and she informs him that they are out for the day.

I huff before finally placing some chicken and rice on my plate, but when I sit down, I just push it around with my fork. My chopsticks are still in their packaging. When I'm in a really good mood, I always attempt using them. Today is not that day.

"Not hungry?" my dad asks.

I lean back in my chair and cross my arms. "I don't feel good."

And it's true. I don't. But it isn't because I feel sick to my stomach.

Everything would all be okay if God would have just made my hair grow back.

Dear Jesus,

To be honest, I don't feel like talking.

Andie

Chapter 5

My Mom Is Too Right

"Hurry up, Andie!" my mom yells down the hall. It's Monday and our homeschool co-op meets at the local community building at nine o'clock. It's ten minutes till. We are running late. Our co-op consists of several families, but my mom leads it up. We are always super early to make sure the classrooms are ready, but not today. My mom had to call Emma's mom this morning to help fill in. I could tell she hated to ask by the millions of apologies she muttered over the phone.

I slept horribly last night. I think it's because I didn't talk to Jesus, but I'm giving Him the silent treatment right now. I've been praying for weeks for my hair to grow faster and all He's given me is a quarter inch. Then there's the tiff Him and I had yesterday while I was standing up in front of everyone at church. Tiff means *quarrel or argument*.

Maybe it wasn't really a tiff, but it sure felt like one to me. I had a problem with the Scripture and since they were God's words, we are most definitely quarreling. Except God hasn't exactly argued with me. It's just me doing all the arguing.

"Andie!" my mom yells again with a little more intensity. The boiling pot is about to spill over. I look at myself one last time in the bathroom mirror, tugging a light pink headband into place. It'll have to do.

I grab my tote bag that I bedazzled last year and sling it over my shoulder. "I'm coming!"

It's just Levi and I that go to homeschool co-op with our mom. Colton already works a job. He's sixteen and our homeschool schedule allows him to work shifts down at the coffee shop other kids his age can't cover. Sometimes when mom takes me downtown when he is working, he sneaks me a small hot chocolate with extra whipped cream.

I hurry out to the garage and climb into our van.

"Feeling better today?" Levi asks with a light smirk on his face.

I glare at him, seeing a fresh new pimple on his nose. I'm going to say something about it, but as if my mom knows my self-control is nonexistent momentarily, she interjects before I get the satisfaction. "Excited for co-op classes today?"

I nod my head but keep my lips glued shut. I think about how supergluing my brother's lips together would be an enjoyable activity.

"Levi?" my mother asks. "What about you?"

I watch my mom studying us in the rearview mirror. She gives me a small smile when she notices me looking at her in the reflection. I look away.

"I guess," he grumbles. He thinks he's too cool for classes. Or really, too cool for anything that doesn't involve a soccer ball.

We get there five minutes after nine o'clock and we scramble out of the van to rush into the building. Everyone stares at us when we hurry in. My mom is all smiles. "Hello, everyone!"

Emma's mom walks up to mine, giving her a hug. "Need any help, Meg?"

"Oh goodness, Marie. You've already done enough by setting up the classrooms. I am so sorry that we are late," my mom mumbles quickly while digging through the large bag she brought with her.

"We're all due some grace, are we not?" Marie asks with a sparkle in her eye.

I locate Emma and see that she's saved a seat for me. Our Monday routine is nearly the same every Monday. We sit together and listen as my mom goes over the weekly announcements and then we listen to a devotional that is usually given by my mom before we all split up going into our individual classes.

I scurry over towards the saved seat and plop down beside Emma with a heavy sigh.

"Everything okay?" Emma asks me.

I shrug my shoulders. "I'm fine."

But I'm not fine and isn't it weird how everyone says they are fine when they clearly are not? I watch my mom do it all the time when she's overwhelmed, or when she's had a bad day. I get so confused why bad days don't seem to be allowed or why we are supposed to act like things don't bother us. And yet, here I am, telling my Sonshine Sister that I am indeed fine, when I'm not.

Emma gives me a look like she knows the truth, but we can't discuss it as my mom clears her throat to begin announcements.

"I am so sorry we are a little late getting started! Do you ever have those mornings where you woke up feeling like you were already behind?" my mom asks, waiting for everyone to give answers. No one did.

"So, it's just me, huh?" she laughs, no nervousness to her tone. She'd been doing this for long enough to feel comfortable in front of other moms and kids, unlike the nerves that were clearly in my tone at church yesterday at the pulpit.

I watch as she shuffles through her papers. It doesn't look like the notes she'd prepared for the devotion today. I had watched her write them down while she had studied her Bible and pulled up some ideas on her phone.

"Well, there's not much to announce so I'm going to dive right into our devotion. I may stumble around a little bit. I threw this together last night," my mom says. I wonder why she felt the need to redo her devotion for the day.

"Have you ever felt angry with God?" she asks.

And there it is. The reason she changed the devotional. She customized it to my very own circumstances. This wasn't the first time she's snuck a lesson into morning devotions when I had to sit there and listen to her. I slouch back in my chair and cross my arms. I feel Emma looking at me.

"Okay, raise your hand if you've been angry with God," my mom instructs, raising her own hand. I watch as moms instantly raise their hands and how several kids slowly admit to their own anger by raising their own. My mom is looking at me with a look that means I better raise my hand because she knows.

I raise my hand reluctantly, trying to discreetly look around hoping no one sees me.

"It's not a sin to be angry at God," my mom explains. "We are human and as humans we often feel a lot of emotions including anger. God clearly made us with the ability to become angry, but it's what we do with our anger. How we respond. I often tell my children that sometimes things happen that are outside of control but what is within our control is how we react. Isn't that right, Andie?"

I feel my cheeks warm, but I nod my head. She isn't wrong and any other day if she had done this devotion, I would have happily agreed with her. Well, most days.

My mom opens her Bible. "Let's read from James, chapter one, verses two through four. Consider it pure joy, my brothers and sisters, whenever you face trials of many kinds, because you know that the testing of your faith produces perseverance. Let perseverance finish its work so that you may be mature and complete, not lacking anything." She pauses before asking, "Does anyone know what perseverance means?"

Emma's hand shoots up in the air.

"Yes, Emma?" my mom calls on her for the answer.

"It means continuing even when there is difficulty or failure," Emma responds with a pleased smile curled around her face.

"Yes! Exactly! We do not quit. We keep going even if what happens isn't what we want. Not everything in this life is going to make us happy. We will be tested in many ways, small ones and big ones.

God is giving you an opportunity to grow your faith. It can be easy to become angry when things feel unfair, or hard, or unhappy. We can blame God for a lot of things. But learning to trust God produces perseverance. Struggles aren't meant to separate you from God, and any anger that comes from those struggles isn't either. It's meant to bring you closer to Him. To find the joy and choose Him, even if we aren't happy with something in our life." My mom smiles at me as she finishes.

Part of me wants to be angry with her, too. I feel like I should make a list with names of those who I'm angry with. But then there is part of me that is thankful she cares enough to take the time to change up her own plans to try to help me.

"So, now I want to ask all of you to think of a time the Lord has been helping you trust Him more. To pray more. To grow closer to Him. I know a couple girls here who have friends that gather to pray more to become more like Jesus." She looks at Emma and me, but I can't look back at my mom. It hurts to realize the truth in what she is saying. I am part of a group that focuses on prayer and I'm currently giving God the silent treatment.

My mom closes with prayer, and I know I should pray, but I'm not ready, yet. I need to talk to God myself, not with my mom and everyone else. Group prayer always makes me think we're all linking up and I'm scared someone will hear my thoughts. But I still join the group in saying, "Amen."

Emma turns to me before heading off to our classroom. "What was that about, Andie? I thought you were just mad at Caroline. Are you mad at God, too?"

"Kind of," I mumble. "I mean, yes. Yes, I am."

Emma nods. "Your hair?"

I bit my lip, embarrassed to admit that I would be angry at God for such a small thing such as my hair.

"It's okay, Andie," Emma says. "I've been mad at God for a lot of different things, but I sure hope you can talk to Him about it. He has good things for you if you'd quit focusing on the things you think are bad."

And I know she meant well and that she was right.

But I still really hated my hair.

Dear Jesus,

I'm still not sure I really want to talk to You. I know I need to, and I also know I owe You an apology, but can I be honest? I'm not ready to say I'm sorry. I mean, it's been six weeks since my really, very bad haircut. I miss my hair and the way I used to look. I know my mom said that I looked like a ragamuffin. Whatever that is? But I miss my ponytails. I promise I'll be better at brushing my knots if I get my hair back. I mean, I probably don't have any right to ask for anything right now, but still...I feel like Samson stripped of his strength. You should understand. You know Samson. If You can, can You ask him how to fix my problems? Surely, he also hated his short hair.

Your Sonshine Sister,

Andie

Chapter 6

I'm like Anne Shirley

"Andie," my mom says through the gap of my bedroom door that's partly open. It's Monday night. The day has been busy. After homeschool co-op, we had lunch with Emma, her mom, and her sisters. Then, I had piano lessons, which I haven't yet decided if I love them or hate them. Perhaps hate is too strong of a word. It should only be reserved for my really, very bad haircut. Levi also had soccer practice, which he claimed was the most important event of the day. It wasn't. At least, not to me.

"Yes, mom," I reply, peeking up from my book I'm reading while situated in a pile of pillows and blankets on my bed.

"I wanted to talk to you about today." When she says those words, my heart drops into my stomach. I feel like a chain is attached to it and it's anchored down within, swimming with the pizza casserole we just consumed for supper.

I nod my head. She makes her way over to my bed, squeezing her way into the pillows and blankets with me.

"Honey, I know you hate your haircut and I'm so sorry that you do. I'm not sure I would have made a different decision as there was no other choice to be had," she mutters, and I can tell she's remembering that fateful day. I'd come downstairs crying because I had worn my hair in a matted ponytail for several days in a row, lying that I had taken a shower. I mean, I think my mom knew, but sometimes I think parents make you learn a lesson instead of fixing the problem. I had tried to brush it out, but it was no use. The knots I had avoided had more than tripled in size.

I nod my head again.

"It's just, when we don't take care of the things we have, those things eventually become a problem. It's like washing the dishes. What would happen if no one around here ever washed the dishes and they continued to pile up in the sink?" she asks me.

"We'd eventually have no dishes," I reply.

"Not only that, but the dirty dishes would start to pile up on the kitchen counters. And soon, it would begin to smell and all the food on the dishes would get crusty and become almost impossible to scrub off," she adds.

I wrinkle my nose at the thought of our kitchen crowded with dirty dishes, imagining them stacked all the way to the ceiling.

"You see, when we just wash our dishes after a meal, it's easier. But if we didn't and we allowed the kitchen to become crowded with dirty dishes, it would feel impossible. It would also be a much bigger problem that we could have prevented with daily care," she explains.

"Just like my hair," I grumble, knowing where she was going with this conversation.

"Exactly. It's important that we take care of the things God gives us," she smiles. "Your hair is a gift, Andie. As is every part of you. God designed you with purpose, even down to each hair follicle. You want to know something?"

I wasn't sure I did, but I nodded again anyways.

"My mom chopped my hair off, too," she mutters. "I thought it was the end of the world. I loved my long hair. It made me feel pretty and yet, I neglected to take care of it. It took forever to brush it. My arm would become tired. So, I just stopped. Then the knots became worse. They really weren't that bad to begin with, but the longer I avoided the problem, the bigger the problem became."

Her words were beginning to sink into my brain.

"So, off with my hair!" she exclaims, which makes my eyebrows shoot up as my eyes expand to the size of large marbles. "Better, than off with my head! Right?"

She laughs to herself, and honestly, I thought the historical joke was funny, too. However, I wasn't ready to give her the satisfaction of my laughter.

"I could list off several excuses if you wanted me to for the decision to take you to Mrs. Lucy and have her cut all the knots out of your hair, but the truth is it simply had to be done, Andie. Your dad and I had to decide on something that we knew you wouldn't be happy with because we knew it was best for you," she says, trying to make it seem as if she had no other choice.

I hadn't realized how mad I was at my mom for taking me to Mrs. Lucy, but I feel my anger surface as my teeth begin to grind.

"I also know you aren't just mad at me. You are angry with God," she adds. I feel shame rush through my veins. It feels like embarrassment is flowing through my body making my shoulders scrunch and my toes curl. "I also know it probably didn't feel good for me to change our devotion to one that felt so personal. We've all been angry with God, Andie. But I wanted to come tell you that I'm sorry."

My head whips up from my sulking into my pillow to look at her. Why was my mom apologizing?

"I should have talked to you about it first before using it as a devotion for everyone," she explains. "I know you are struggling right now, and I just didn't know how best to help you in your struggle. And honestly, I kind of allowed myself to become irritated about the way you have been handling the hair situation. But that's not my place. It's my place to try to help you through your problems, however you need to process them and however long it takes."

I want to say something, but no words come to my lips. I feel like she's had this talk prepared and I have had no time to prepare my response.

"I love you, Andie," my mom says. "So, very much. God has given me such a gift in you, Levi, and Colton. It's also a responsibility that I hope you'll understand one day. Motherhood is beautiful and messy. Much like your hair once was."

She smiles at me, but I'm not quite ready for the hair joke.

"I love you, too," I mutter, refusing to give her a smile. I don't want her to think everything is okay now, but I also know how much she loves me. Even if I still disagree with her decision to ask Mrs. Lucy to take scissors to my hair and chop it into some kind of clunky bob that makes me feel like an alien with a toupee. A toupee is *a wig of sorts created to cover a bald spot*. I won't even give my hair the satisfaction of calling it a complete wig. It's too sparse in my opinion.

She snuggles down beside me. "So, what are you reading?"

"Anne of Green Gables," I mumble.

"Oh, one of my favorites!" she exclaims. "Did you know Marilla had to cut off Anne's hair, too?"

I rolled my eyes. I knew. When you were in mourning for your own hair, how did you not think about all your favorite characters and the same disasters they've been through? Anne felt much distress over her short hair, mirroring my own agony. Agony is just a *better way to say pain*. It's at the very least, more dramatic.

"Except, she dyed her hair," my mom continues. "She wasn't happy with her red hair, wanting it to be what she believed a much more beautiful alternative in raven black. But then, it turned green instead. Sometimes what we think is better is not always best."

I sigh into my pillow, wanting to bury myself underneath it to muffle my mom's ramblings. I know all of this. It is one of my favorite books.

"So, Marilla cut it short. In fact, I believe the book says, *unfashionably short*. Short hair was embarrassing back then. Not anymore, though. Lots of girls have short hair," she rambles on and all I can think is that none of my own friends have short hair. I'm the first Sonshine Sister with short hair, and I don't like it one bit.

In fact, I very much feel like Anne Shirley. When Anne's hair had to be cut off and she handed Marilla the scissors, she said she felt her heart was broken. Then when she saw herself in the mirror, she called herself ugly.

I didn't want to say it out loud, but I feel the very same way as Anne Shirley.

Dear Jesus,

I've decided I can talk to You. I mean, I know I talked to You earlier, but I was just rambling my thoughts. I wasn't really talking to You. I know my hair is my fault. No one tied the knots in my hair, although I still believe You could have unknotted them like my dad untangles my necklaces. Maybe there is a lesson here, like with Anne Shirley. Maybe my hair wasn't green, but it was a problem. My mom said when we don't take care of a problem it can become a bigger problem. I suppose that is true. But Jesus, I hate my hair. I feel ugly and I feel like I look ugly ~~expecially~~ especially compared to my Sonshine Sisters. I know I'm not supposed to compare myself to them, but they are so pretty with their long hair. Oh, and I'm sorry.

Your Sonshine Sister,

Andie

Chapter 7

An Unaccepted Apology

I'm looking at the dark green door in front of me. I glance down at my new boots my mom bought me yesterday at the thrift store. They are shiny black and even have a small heel which made me squeal with glee when my mom agreed that I could have them. They were a rare find as they looked like they had never been worn.

But even the thrill of the new boots couldn't lift my spirits at this moment. I need to apologize to Caroline for my outburst last Saturday. Apologies are so hard. Especially when I still think I'm right.

I knock on the door and send up a silent prayer that Caroline isn't home, but unfortunately, she opens the door immediately. I look up at her, taking in the unusual sight of her hair flowing down around her shoulders. It's incredibly long and as black and shiny as my boots. It's the kind of hair Anne Shirley wanted, and I understand why. It's beautiful.

"I wondered if you were actually going to knock," she grumbles. "I've been watching you from the window."

A sheepish grin stretches over my lips. I learned this week during my vocabulary lesson that sheepish means *showing embarrassment from shame or lack of self-confidence*. I have a lot of sheepishness these days. Caroline's hair let down from her normal tight bun isn't helping either.

"Can I talk to you?" I ask politely and quietly.

"I suppose," she mutters, stepping out of the way so I can enter her house.

It's a beautiful house. I've always loved it. They have a grand foyer that even has a massive crystal chandelier. Before we became the Sonshine Sisters, when we were much younger, we used to dress up and pretend that this foyer was a ballroom. Her mom would make us cupcakes and little PB&J sandwiches cut up in triangles. We'd play classical music and curtsy to one another. Okay, so maybe it wasn't when we were much younger. It was two years ago.

"I feel awful for the way I acted at our last meeting," I say, and I do feel awful for the way I acted. That part is true. I threw a temper tantrum, those things that both babies, adults, and evidently ten-year-olds can do.

She stands in front of me, her arms crossed. Caroline is slender and taller than I am. She practices ballet daily and always seems to be put together perfectly, but today she's wearing a baggy T-shirt and a pair of shorts that looks like something my brother would wear to soccer practice.

She says nothing in response.

"I mean, can I be honest with you, Caroline?" I ask. The Sonshine Sisters vowed to always be honest with one another. Although, I'm not sure we always were. Sometimes it was hard to be honest when you were dealing with hard things.

She pulls her lips together in a tight fish face. She looks ridiculous but I know she's just being stubborn.

I proceed with my explanation even though she doesn't answer my question. "I don't understand your obsession with boys. I think they are gross. Repulsive, at times, even."

She rolls her eyes before finally answering, "And I don't know why you act so dramatically about your hair. It's short. So what?"

"So what?!" I spit. "How would you feel if your mom had your hair chopped off today?"

"She wouldn't," she replies coolly. "I brush mine."

It hurts so much to have this conversation and for her to refuse to see my own pain in this situation. Or maybe it was even worse? Maybe she did see my pain and she was pouring salt onto my wound, which is just a weird way of saying she already knew I was hurting but wanted to hurt me even more.

"I came over here to say that I'm sorry," I cry. "To try to explain myself, even if you didn't understand. My mom told me that a problem becomes an even bigger problem when we avoid it. I know we have a problem, but you obviously do not want to fix it."

"I don't have a problem," Caroline mumbles. "You do."

I turn away from her, tears brimming in my eyes, but before I leave, I make sure to say the last words. "Pride comes before the fall."

It's a popular saying among us who love Jesus, but it's also not very nice for me to say to Caroline right now. I know that, but she's hurt me. It comes from a popular verse in Proverbs where it warns that a haughty attitude, or *being stuck-up*, comes before we are humbled. Humbled means *we understand that we are not more important than others*. At least, that's what my mom told me when I asked.

So, basically, I just told Caroline that she's a stuck-up snob and she'd find out eventually that she's no better than I am.

I shut the front door behind me and then stomp down the sidewalk back to my own house. I let my stomps fuel my anger. I open our cheerful yellow front door, which is so much better than Caroline's ugly green one, and then I let out a yell. "Ughhhhhhh!"

My mom comes running out from the kitchen, hands covered in slimy dough. "What's the matter, Andie?"

"Girls are the worst!" I scream. And it's funny when you really think about it. I went over to apologize to my friend but not give up my opinion that boys are impossibly horrible, and Caroline had just proved that girls can be horrible, too. Maybe she deserved to be obsessed with the strange creatures.

I hear a faint, "Amen!", from down the hallway and I know Levi is chuckling to himself in his room at my outburst.

"What happened?" my mom asks gently. She knew I had gone over to try to amend things from Saturday.

"I tried to apologize, mom." Tears begin trickling down my face rapidly. "I told her I still didn't understand her obsession with boys. She told me obsessing with my hair was stupid and that it wouldn't have ever happened to her because she brushes her hair."

My mom wraps me in an awkward hug as she attempts to embrace me with her elbows, so she doesn't get the sticky dough in my hair or on my clothes. I appreciate her efforts. I imagine that the dough would stick in my hair like bubblegum, and I'd have to buzz it all off.

"Oh, honey," she says. "I'm so sorry."

And I know she is. I stuff myself into her body that smells like brown sugar, patchouli, and now yeast. I let my tears soak her apron and even use it as a tissue to wipe the snot from my nose that has also started to rapidly pour out yellow gunk.

I finally pull away and say, "You should probably wash that."

I help her out of the frilly apron, balling it up to take it to the laundry room.

"Would you like to come help me with shaping the bread loaves?" she asks.

Of course, I do. Cooking is basically my love language, whatever that was. My parents spoke of love languages often, but I still didn't fully understand what it meant. I had just heard them say things like, *"Tacos are my love language"* or *"Coffee is my love language"*, so I figured cooking could be mine.

"I'll go start this in the wash first," I say.

She smiles warmly at me. "Thanks, Andie."

I stuff the apron into the washing machine, deciding a hot wash is in need thanks to my germs now smeared all over my mom's favorite apron. It was a gift from my dad. The apron had bright flowers all over it with frilly pink lace stitched practically everywhere. I wore it every Tuesday for my kitchen night. It kind of felt like the princess ball gown of aprons.

I return to the kitchen to see that my mom is kneading the bread dough.

"Would you like to knead for a while?" she questions.

Yes, I definitely want to punch the fluffy ball of flour, yeast, and water. Baking bread was the baker's equivalent of an athlete with boxing gloves. Except those who baked, got to eat delicious, warm bread afterwards.

"Put me in coach!" I exclaim and my mom laughs.

Even though I don't like sports, sometimes I use sports references that I hear during my brother's soccer games or practices. The varied vocabulary is especially handy at times.

I'm punching the dough when my mom asks, "So, what about Saturday?"

And I hate the thought of Saturday and having to face Caroline at our Sonshine Sister Club meeting. I can't imagine it'll be good. In fact, I figure it'll be extremely uncomfortable.

"I don't know," I mumble.

"Maybe she'll be ready to listen then?" my mom suggests.

I bite my lip knowing I need to tell my mom what else I told Caroline, but I'm also embarrassed to admit to it. "I kind of said something else."

My mom places her elbows onto the counter, resting her face in her palms. She's staring straight at me, and I imagine that all time has stopped, even our breathing has seized. We are statues in our kitchen that can only come back to life with me admitting to my mistake.

"Pride comes before the fall," I ramble quickly, hoping that the faster the words come out of my mouth the less they will hurt.

My mom nods her head. "Well, you aren't wrong, but you also weren't right."

I feel my cheeks warm as I begin to shape the dough into a round loaf. "But she was being prideful."

"I didn't say she wasn't. You were right, but you were wrong in pointing it out in that moment," my mom says.

"Then when is the right time to point it out?" I question, as I pat at the loaf.

"When you can say it in love instead of in spite," my mom answers.

Spite means *I said it with the intention to hurt or offend*, and well, I did. I wanted her to hurt like she had hurt me. It wasn't the right thing to say and honestly, it didn't feel good saying it either. Well, maybe it had when I first said it. But now all I feel is regret.

Almost as much as I regret not brushing my hair more often.

Dear Jesus,

I tried to apologize to Caroline. What happens when someone doesn't want your apology? Do I still need to apologize? Does she need to apologize? I'm not looking forward to Saturday. I know Caroline will glare at me. What if she says other things that are mean? Being 10 sometimes just stinks, Jesus.

Your Sonshine Sister,

Andie

Chapter 8
Lies, Lies, and Lessons

"I'm President!" Sam screams as she enters my room with a mouth full of teeth and squeals. I'm not sure I've ever seen anyone smile bigger.

I jump up from the floor and join her squeals, my room becoming an echo chamber of high-pitched excitement. We grab each other's hands and hold on tight as we do a little rendition of *the jive,* which is a very happy, energetic dance that was created sometime in the 1930's to accompany jazz music. Which is not my favorite music, or really the favorite music of any of the Sonshine Sisters. We usually play some kind of pop tune that thoroughly irritates my brothers if we play it too loudly.

"Congratulations!" I shriek. "You are the perfect girl for the job!"

Soon Emma and Sarah peek their heads into my room, their eyes all wide with interest in what has just taken place.

"What's all this about?" Emma asks.

"I was voted in President of my class!" Sam announces.

If the screams were loud the first time, they are even louder now. I wonder if my bedroom window can shatter from such a shrill sound. I imagine the glass panes are vibrating, syncing up to a beat of everyone's feet that are erratically stomping on my floor. Even the carpet isn't padded enough to muffle the sound.

"Congrats, Sam!" Emma says as she throws her arms around her neck in a hug.

Sarah and I lean in around them.

"Where's Caroline?" I ask.

We pull apart from the tangle that probably resembled a knot I once had in my hair. Sarah looks at me with an expression that lets me know she doesn't want to say what she'd been asked to.

"She's not coming," Sarah mumbles.

"Is she sick?" Sam questions.

"Not exactly." Sarah looks down at the floor. "She said she isn't coming because she doesn't want to see Andie."

Emma and Sam turn to look at me and I wish I could melt into the fibers of my carpet. I don't want to have this conversation with the other Sonshine Sisters. Of course, for all they know it could only be about our meeting last Saturday.

"She says you came and saw her on Thursday," Sarah adds.

Well, now they know it was more than just last Saturday. Every part of me wants to defend myself and say awful things about Caroline but instead I just burst into tears. The ugly kind that wrinkles your face into all sorts of weird shapes and colors.

"Oh, Andie!" Sam exclaims. She's the first to wrap her arms around me as I crumple to the floor. She crumples alongside me.

"What happened?" Emma asks, concern scrunching in her eyebrows as she looks at me. She kneels down in front of me.

Sarah is the last one standing, as if she doesn't know if she should be sad for me when she's talked to Caroline. It makes me wonder what Caroline has said. Did she make it sound worse than it was? Did she make it seem like she wasn't rude that day, too?

"I tried to apologize," I manage to say between my cries that had become hiccups. "I told her I still didn't like boys and didn't understand why she did. Then, she told me that she didn't understand why I was so upset about my hair. When I asked how she would feel if all hers was cut off she told me that wouldn't happen because she brushes her hair."

I pause, looking up at Sarah to see how she is responding. She's looking at her feet again.

"I told her I was there to say that I was sorry for how I acted because I knew we had a problem. She told me she didn't have a problem. I did." I stumble over the rest of it, trying to decide if I tell the whole truth or leave out the last part. If I told them what I said, would they stop feeling sorry for me? Would they then feel sorry for her?

I decide that I need to tell them the truth.

"Then before I left, I told her that pride comes before the fall," I mumble quickly. "I shouldn't have said it. I know I shouldn't. But I was so hurt. I felt like she was trying to hurt me, and I wanted to hurt her back."

"Oh, Andie," Sam soothed. "We all say things we don't mean to say sometimes. We all do it."

"Sam's right," Emma adds. "Just last week I told my sister she was the most annoying creature ever to crawl the planet. Even though, I know you understand how annoying siblings can be, it wasn't nice for me to say."

I look up at Sarah. She finally looks down at me. "That's not what Caroline said."

"But that's what happened," I say, confused by what Sarah is saying. I didn't leave any part out, not even what I wanted to.

"She says you came over and told her how dumb she was for liking boys," Sarah mutters, her arms crossed. "She says that you said you understood why boys didn't like her, either."

"None of that is true!" I shout. "The only thing I said about boys was that I personally thought they were repulsive. We didn't even discuss whether boys liked her or not."

I am angry that Caroline would lie about our conversation to another Sonshine Sister and add pieces that weren't even said at all.

Sarah shrugs her shoulders. "That's what she told me."

"It may be what she told you, but it isn't what happened," I stammer in disbelief.

"Okay," Sam interjects. "The only way we can figure out what is going on is if we get to hear both sides. We are the Sonshine Sisters. We are supposed to want to become more like Jesus and help each other become more like Jesus."

And she's right, but I feel so betrayed right now. Caroline made it seem like words came out of my mouth that never did. I said something that I regret but I didn't say all those things. And now, my Sonshine Sisters are confused as to what is true.

I want everyone to leave but we haven't even started our meeting.

"Do you think you can convince Caroline to come over?" Emma asks Sarah.

Sarah shakes her head. "She's not coming."

"Well, we have some extra things to pray over this week," Sam says. "Let's get started."

Sam pulls out her sparkly notebook and I watch as she quietly draws a heart beside her answered prayer of becoming President. I feel horrible that the night we should be celebrating our Sonshine Sister and her answered prayer, has turned into a night of confusion and cheerlessness.

I want to say something to make it better, but I can't think of what to say. Everything in my head feels heavy and mixed up.

"Answered prayers?" Sam asks.

My room is quiet.

"Prayer requests?" Sam asks.

"Gus has a cold. He's all sniffly. Mom said he just needs a little time to get over it," Emma says.

I watch Sam write down Emma's request for her dog, Gus.

"I have my first volleyball game next week," Sarah says. "It's just recreational right now, but I'm hoping the extra practice and experience will help me make the team next year."

I watch as Sam writes down Sarah's request for her volleyball game.

"I have a pre-algebra test next week," Sam says as she scribbles her own prayer request into the notebook. "It's one of the harder courses I'm taking this year. My mom thought it would possibly be a little overwhelming for me. I don't want to prove her right, even though it really has been difficult."

Then Sam looks over at me.

I shrug my shoulders. "For this really, very bad haircut to stop making everything in my life worse."

Sam smiles at me. It's one of those small smiles that means she cares, even if it isn't something she personally cares about. It's what us Sonshine Sisters are supposed to do. Then I realize I haven't truly acted like I care about anything my Sonshine Sisters have cared about lately, besides Sam getting President. But everything else I had made into background noise in my life—all chatter and no cares.

I realize how selfish I've been.

When Sam prays over everything I cry while everyone else has their eyes closed.

Dear Jesus,

I'm so hurt and confused. I don't know why Caroline would lie about me. You've been betrayed before. I mean, Your betrayal was worse, for sure. I'm not trying to compare. I just know You know that it doesn't feel good.

I also feel so selfish, Jesus. I've cared so much about my hair that I've forgotten to care about other things my friends care about. Please, help me. I don't know how to not care about my hair. It still makes me not feel like myself. I feel like some weird, awful version of me.

Your Sonshine Sister,

Andie

Chapter 9

Dooms Day

I have dreaded this day for a while now, but it's finally here. Family pictures.

My mom is insistent every fall that we have photos taken when the colors change from their greens to oranges. It's her favorite season and she commemorates it with many things. Pumpkin Spice lattes as soon as Sam's mom will carry the syrup down at the coffee shop, wearing sweaters until you must peel them off soaked from sweat when the summer heat zaps you in the afternoon because it's not truly autumn yet, and the dreaded family pictures.

Now, I haven't always felt disdain for them. Disdain means a *feeling of dislike.* But this year our family pictures will feature my short hair, and these are the photos that get plastered on our Christmas cards. Every family member and friend across the country will put this photo up on a wall or a refrigerator. My really, very bad haircut will be displayed for all to see. I've been able to avoid the embarrassment of my face being shared on my mom's Facebook since the snipping. I had forgotten about family pictures. All my efforts to avoid the camera were for nothing.

The outfit my mom bought for me is laying on my bed. It's a dark orange sweater dress with plaid tights to go underneath. She was even able to locate a fabric that somewhat matched the plaid on the tights and fashioned a headband for me. I don't mind the matching, but my brothers complain every year. It's usually fun to watch them do something mom likes and they do not. Except for this year, I will join their sulking.

"We leave in fifteen minutes!" I hear my dad shout.

I drag myself to my bed to transfer the outfit to my body. I pull the sweater dress over my head feeling my hair frizz before my head pops out of the tunnel of fabric that seems five feet long.

When it does, I can tell my hair is standing on its ends before I even glance into my mirror.

"Great," I mumble. As if short hair wasn't bad enough, let's make it look like I stuck my finger into an electrical socket. I wonder if that might be a better alternative to family pictures, but quickly shake the idea away. Electrocution is probably not my best idea.

I jump and dance around my room as I wiggle the tights over my legs. At least they will cover the bruises from all the soccer balls my shins took this last week. I have tried to do my best since our last Sonshine Sister meeting to care about the things that the people I love care about. Yes, this even includes Levi. He needed someone to practice with and Colton was busy working a few extra shifts at the coffee shop. My mom won't play soccer. She says she has bad knees. I think that's just her adult excuse of getting out of having to take the hits from the soccer ball, which I did.

I also helped Emma give medicine to her dog, Gus, and went to Sarah's first volleyball game.

I suppose I should choose to care more about these pictures for my mom, but this one involves my hair and I'm just not quite ready yet. She did mention that she was supposed to help me through my problems in my own timing. So, I'm declaring that it isn't the right time.

I get the tights shimmied over my bottom half, pull my sweater dress back down, and when I look in the mirror, I'm not sure how to remedy the unsightly scene that is my hair.

"Mom!" I yell, irritation swirling alongside my cries.

My door swings open. "Yes, Andie?"

"My hair," I mumble. "It's awful. I don't know what to do."

"Where's your brush?" she asks. I point to my desk where the pink paddle of needles lies. She swiftly retrieves it and makes her way to where I sit slumped on my bed. She begins to gently sweep the brush through my hair.

"Do we have to do this today?" I complain, already feeling how itchy the tights are on my thighs.

"Yes, Andie," she replies. "Caroline's mom has had us on her schedule for months."

My stomach turns. How did I forget that Caroline's mom was the photographer for these? She'd just started up her photography business a couple years ago. Last year was our first family pictures taken by her, but everything had been fine between Caroline and I then.

I become lost in my own fears and anxiousness. What has Caroline told her mom? Will her mom treat me any differently?

I feel the fabric hug against my scalp as my mom carefully wiggles the headband into place, pulling a few strands of hair to fall around my face. It's been eight weeks since the unfortunate chopping. It's grown some, but not enough. The bob doesn't tickle my jawline, instead it curls around it.

"Perfect," my mom beams with satisfaction as she stares at me with a smile. I cringe under her adjective usage, because I'm looking in the mirror and still feeling like Anne Shirley with her short hair. Last year my mom styled my hair in two beautiful braids that framed my face perfectly. I miss those braids.

I pull on my boots and look one last time in the mirror. Yep. I definitely miss my braids.

I drag my feet on the carpet as I make my way to the living room. Everyone is waiting for me. My brothers are dressed in matching button-ups that feature a deep green that is also featured in my tights and headband. My dad is wearing a black shirt with a tie that matches my headband. My mom may have gone too far with her matching and crafting. I look over at my mom, applying a last swipe of lip gloss. She's dressed in an orange dress like mine, but even though we match I like hers better. Her dark hair is out of her usual messy bun and curled around her shoulders.

"Let's go Wilson Crew!" my dad announces, pushing himself up from the couch.

"Oh, Daniel!" my mom exclaims. "You've wrinkled your shirt."

She rushes over to tug and pull at the back of my dad's shirt while he is giving me a look of innocence—his eyebrows raised up high and a slight shrug to his shoulders. I giggle quietly.

We are meeting Caroline's mom at the park. Newport has a large park. It has walking paths, a park just for dogs, a couple different places filled with playground equipment, and a ballfield. It is dense with trees. Dense means *there is a lot of matter in one small space*. So, basically the park is packed with trees, and they are currently all turning from green to orange and red.

We load up in the van, my mom lecturing us to be careful how we sit so we do not wrinkle our clothes like our dad has done. Mom becomes prickly like a cactus on picture day. She always claims she loves our family pictures and yet, she sure acts like she doesn't enjoy the process.

We arrive at the park in minutes, unloading and being inspected by our mom.

I watch as she tugs at Colton's shirt, straightening it into what she thinks is good enough. He's so much taller than her but mirrors her in many ways. His dark hair matches hers and their eyes are both brown with a slight green twinkle in them. Mom calls it hazel.

"Mom," Colton says. "Take a breath. It's just family pictures."

She gives him a small smile while she looks up at him. "I know."

The last two years I've watched their relationship as mother and son change. He's gotten older and with it, he's become a lot less annoying than my other brother, Levi. Levi, who is currently balancing a soccer ball on his head.

"Levi!" my mom exclaims. "You are going to mess up your hair!"

He sends her a sly smile as if he knew it was going to irritate her. I watch my mom give my dad 'the look'. It's the look that means he better do something because she's about to lose it. By lose it, I mean yell. Sometimes my mom did yell, and then she'd cry and apologize to all of us later for allowing her emotions to control her words and actions.

My dad pulls Levi to the side, quickly removing the ball from his head. He's whispering in his ear, but I can't hear if my dad is giving Levi a lecture or if he's reminding Levi to stay in my mom's good graces for the day.

"You look beautiful, Andie," my mom gushes as she looks over me, crouching down to separate my sweater dress that has become suctioned to my tights.

I try to believe her. I close my eyes and imagine that what my mom says is true, but I just can't do it.

I hear the crunch of gravel as Caroline's mom pulls up next to our van. She rushes out. "I'm so sorry! I am running behind!"

"Oh, Lisa! You aren't late at all," my mom reassures, hurrying over to help her with anything she may need to unload.

"Meg!" Lisa exclaims. "Your family just looks perfect. I love the outfits you picked out. Perfect for a Christmas card photo!"

My face drops along with my stomach at the reminder that this haircut would be forever etched into everyone's memories as the photo was sent out all over the world. Well, maybe just a few states, but it sure felt like the world.

"Oh, look at you, Andie!" Lisa croons. "I just love how your headband matches your tights. And that haircut. I still love it. It's so you!"

Her tone and words seem genuine, as if Caroline hasn't said anything about our fight or lied about what I said.

"Thank you," I mutter.

"I tried to get Caroline to come today," she says. "But she was insistent she needed to practice a new ballet move for Monday's class. I don't know what has happened since school has started but she's become a different girl."

I wonder what she means by that, but I don't have time to ask as she begins to gather all of us up to make a short trek across the park to where she has decided is the picture-perfect spot.

Twenty minutes of excruciating pain making sure I plaster a smile upon my face, and we are finally done. I try to relax my cheek muscles, but they feel stuck in place.

I stand by my mom as my dad and brothers lightly kick around the soccer ball, no longer restrained by my mom's expectations for perfection. Lisa is talking about Caroline, and I lean in a little closer to try to hear their conversation.

"I don't know what is going on, Meg," Lisa says. "Something seems wrong. She isn't acting like herself. She's been going to school in baggy sweats and her hair undone. She's always begged for the latest styles and keeps her hair tight and high in a bun."

"Maybe middle school is more stressful than she's letting on?" my mom suggests.

"I've talked to her teachers," Lisa answers. "They say her efforts towards her schoolwork haven't changed, but they have also noticed the change in her physical appearance and demeanor. They say she doesn't talk to many other students. She keeps to herself, and that is very unlike her."

I try to keep up with their words reminding myself that demeanor means *behavior that you can see.* Caroline has always been extremely outgoing. She loves people and people usually love her.

"Is it a boy?" my mom asks, and I silently gag at the idea of it. I can't imagine changing my whole personality because of a boy, but this is Caroline they are talking about.

"She won't say," Lisa mutters. Her words seem heavy as they drop from her mouth. "She's not talking much to me or to Carl. We don't know what to do."

My mom puts her arm around Lisa and Lisa leans into her.

"Would Andie know anything?" Lisa asks.

I worry about what my mom will say. She knows everything. Will she tell Lisa that we had a fight?

"I'll talk to Andie," my mom answers. "Maybe she can help."

"Thank you, Meg," Lisa whispers. I can barely hear her words, but I can sense some relief, as if she was grateful for any help.

But the part she doesn't know about is I'm not sure how I can help. Caroline currently hates me.

Later that night, my mom excitedly swings my bedroom door open while I'm reading in bed.

"Andie!" she squeals. "Lisa just sent me a sneak peek of the photos from today! You have to see!"

She shoves her cell phone in my hand, and I look at the screen that is bigger than my palm. The colors are vibrant. The trees are the perfect colors of autumn but with plush green grass beneath our feet. The greens and oranges of our clothes mimic the greens and oranges of the scenery. All five of us are smiling. I'm even smiling. Smiling with my really, very bad haircut.

I plaster another fake smile on my face. "This is great, mom."

I do my best to care about what she cares about even though I'm thinking that this picture is a lie. Everyone is going to look at it and think I'm happy about my hair when I'm not.

Dear Jesus,

Something is going on with Caroline. I know You know what it is but it seems to be a mystery to everyone else. Maybe that's why she's been so terrible to me? I mean, I know I haven't been nice either BUTTTT I didn't tell lies. Not that I'm keeping track of sins, Jesus, or that one is worse than the other. I know all sins are sins. But You know what I mean. Right?

Also, can You somehow make Caroline's mom lose the photo files? My mom will be devastated but something must be done about the fact that everyone will believe I'm happy with my hair.

Your Sonshine Sister,

Andie

Chapter 10

Hurt People, Hurt People

It's Saturday, and I'm bravely standing in front of Caroline's house once again. Not because I necessarily want to, but because my mom has insisted that Caroline needs a Sonshine Sister to get to the bottom of whatever is going on with her. I don't know why it must be me. I'm pretty sure Sarah, Emma, or Sam would be a better choice for this, but they aren't the ones looking at the green front door that is now adorned with a wreath that has a million mini pumpkins glued on it.

I'll admit that it is cute. It's not the traditional autumn colors but instead all the pumpkins are colored in pastel shades of the rainbow.

I finally gain the gumption to knock on the door. Gumption means *to have the energy and determination one needs to do what needs to be done.*

Fortunately, it isn't Caroline who greets me, but her mom.

"Oh, Andie! How wonderful of you to stop by!" she gushes. And I know this visit isn't a surprise by her tone. My mom must have texted her.

"Hi, Mrs. Johnson," I say politely. "I love the wreath on your door."

"Aw, thanks, Andie," she beams, but I can still see the concern behind her brown eyes. Concern she has for her daughter and she's hoping I can help. I feel useless. "I'll take you to Caroline."

"Does she know I'm here?" I question.

"Caroline loves surprises," she says, and while I know that is usually true, I'm not like all the good surprises Caroline loves. I'm not a Frappuccino from the coffee shop, or a new scrunchie to wear around her ballet bun, or the newest shade of nail polish. I'm Andie, the girl she currently doesn't want to see. Seeing me will be like finding a long strand of hair in your meal at a restaurant, or finding a mouse running around your bedroom, or discovering your brother took the last chocolate chip pancake.

I'm not a good surprise.

"Caroline!" her mom exclaims. "Look who came by to see you!"

Her bedroom door is open revealing a room full of baby pink and reflections. Her dad built her a wall of mirrors last year along with a barre so she could practice ballet to her heart's content. That means *being able to do what you love to do for as long as you want to do it.*

She looks up from her bed, scowling at me. She's wearing a set of gray sweats that I've never even known her to own. Her hair is down, and dare I say…knotted?! What's happened to Caroline?

I watch as she forces an uncomfortable looking smile on her face. "Hi, Andie."

"I'll leave you two," her mom mutters as she closes the door behind her. Great, I'm left with this sulking, seething version of Caroline that is more like a monster than a girl.

"Hi, Caroline," I mumble.

She glares at me one more time before looking down at her lap. She's got her legs pretzeled.

"Caroline, I wanted to apologize for how I left things last time," I say, even though every part of me wants to yell at her for lying about me. She's obviously going through something. "It was rude of me to say what I did before I left."

Silence.

How was I supposed to help her if she wasn't going to add to this conversation? I stand awkwardly in the middle of her room, catching my reflection in her mirror. I wore my hair half up today. Mom had helped me brush it up into a small ponytail. It doesn't look great, but it doesn't look horrible either.

"Your hair has grown," Caroline finally says, even though it's barely a whisper.

"A bit," I eagerly say, glad she's added to the conversation. "I only need about twelve more inches."

I smile at her, but she doesn't smile back. She looks as if all joy has evaporated out of her body leaving this alien of flesh and bone dressed up in boring sweats behind.

"What's wrong, Caroline?" The question leaves my lips before I can think if it's the best time to ask.

She grimaces at the words. A grimace is *kind of like a scowl except it looks as if the person who gave it just twisted their face into a look of disgust or pain,* but sometimes it can be done out of fun. I've grimaced many times at my brother when he's made gross jokes that I think are hilarious. Caroline's grimace is not one she's made because she thinks this situation is funny.

I may as well go all in now, so I ask the question I've been wanting to. "Why did you lie about what I said to Sarah?"

Another grimace.

"It was hurtful, Caroline," I continue. "I love you very much as a Sonshine Sister but that wasn't a very Sonshine Sister thing to do. I know I was wrong, too, but when Sarah told us what you had told her, I couldn't understand why you would tell her things I never said."

And then it happens. She bursts into tears. The kind you picture in books where they lift their head up and supernatural, gigantic drops of water erupt from their eyes like geysers sending jets of water into the air. Accompanying the waterworks is a noise that makes your eardrums wish they'd cease to work as you cringe at the sound that is exploding from Caroline's mouth.

I rush to her side, pulling her into me. I pat her arm. She keeps crying.

Finally, she wipes the snot that is also streaming alongside her tears with the sleeve of her sweatshirt and turns to look at me. "I'm so sorry, Andie. Middle school is a nightmare. It's been awful and because of it I've been awful, too."

"What's going on?" I ask, genuine concern in my question.

"The girls are so mean," she mumbles. "I tried to make friends with some of the older girls hoping that would give me a better chance at getting noticed by Matthew. They pretended to be my friends. I did everything to please them, and then they laughed at me. Not with me. At me. They made fun of my body, my nose, and my feelings for Matthew in FRONT OF HIM. I didn't know what to do. I stood there frozen with no friends by my side as these girls and Matthew laughed at me."

"What do you mean they made fun of your body and your nose?" I ask. I'm confused by what she is saying. I think Caroline is beautiful.

"Older girls are vicious, Andie," she cries. "They pick you apart trying to find all your imperfections so they can feel better about theirs. They are older so...you know...some of them have curves."

And then it hits me. Did they make fun of Caroline because she hasn't hit puberty yet? I knew some things about puberty. My mom has sat me down a few times, and then there is the fact that I have two older brothers. Their puberty is different, but overall it sounds like an awful time.

"There is nothing wrong with you, Caroline," I say confidently because I know there isn't. "Remember, God made you wonderfully and fearfully. He calls you beautiful."

Then Caroline cries more tears as she nods her head. "I know, but sometimes it doesn't feel that way."

And I know how she feels. I haven't felt wonderful or beautiful, either.

"I'm sorry," I say. "I'm sorry the girls are mean and I'm sorry that they said awful things in front of the boy you like."

I mean it, too, even though I still don't understand boys.

"I don't like him anymore," Caroline mumbles. "I can't like someone who makes fun of me."

And I'm glad she knows that. Boys should stand up for others when they are being torn down. Girls should, too. My mom's voice is constantly repeating in my head about how we have the choice to build others up or tear others down. She says this to my brothers and I almost daily and has for the last several years.

"He should have stood up for you," I add.

She nods her head. I look over at her hair.

"Your hair, Caroline," I sigh. "You have tangles and knots."

Another tear slips down her cheek. I'm not sure how she has any left to cry. "I haven't let my mom help me."

I give a small smile. "She's worried about you, you know?"

She nods her head again. "I'm sorry, Andie. I'm so sorry I lied about what you said. I wanted Sarah to feel sorry for me and...I even did it to hurt you. I knew it would. I wanted someone else to be hurt like I was."

Her face flushes as the words come out. She is embarrassed about the way she acted but I also understand. "Hurt people, hurt people," I whisper.

"What?" she asks.

"Hurt people, hurt people," I repeat but a little louder. "My dad has told me this many times. Sometimes when we are hurting, our instinct is to hurt others, too. It's why I said what I did when I left your house. I wanted you to hurt after you had hurt me."

"But it's not what Jesus would do," Caroline says, her shoulders falling with disappointment.

"No, it isn't," I agree. "But we can both choose to do better now."

Finally, Caroline smiles for the first time. "We can do better."

"Where is your brush and detangling spray?" I ask.

"What?" she questions.

"I'm going to help you tame this mess before you end up like me. I don't want you to have to chop all your hair off, too! It'll be forever before you can put it in a bun again," I explain.

She jumps off her bed and retrieves both items for me, but before she hands them over, she says, "It wouldn't be so bad to look like you, Andie."

And it seems genuine. Maybe, just maybe, my hair wasn't as much of a disaster as I've made it out to be.

Dear Jesus,

Middle School sounds awful and I'm so glad I only have one annoying seventh grader to deal with, and that he's my brother. I feel so bad for Caroline. Why are those girls so mean? I would ask for revenge, but I know that's not my place, so I'm going to ask for change, Jesus. Please change the hearts of the girls and of Matthew so they want to become more like You, too. And help Caroline and I do better. We sure made a mess of things with our problems. It just goes to show that we are all going through things that sometimes we don't know about.

And thank You for a good meeting with the Sonshine Sisters tonight. It was good to have Caroline back.

Your Sonshine Sister,

Andie

Chapter 11

A Blushing Brother

Colton is bringing a girl home tonight for our family supper. It was a surprise to me, but my mom just beamed and gave him a little wink when he asked if Laura could join us for our Sunday night meal. I should have known mom knew about her already. Moms know everything.

I've never met her before. She doesn't go to our church, and she isn't homeschooled. She goes to the same private school Sam goes to though, so I'm asking Sam about her after our church service.

"Who's the mystery lady?" Levi asks while elbowing Colton in the side. Normally Colton would have elbowed him back, rammed him into a wall, or tossed him onto the couch, but instead he blushes. MY BROTHER BLUSHES!

"Her name is Laura," Colton replies softly. I could tell he liked this girl, and that this supper was important to him.

"I'm excited to meet her," I say, smiling at my oldest brother.

"I think you'll like her, Andie," he replies, pulling me in close for a side hug. He started voluntarily hugging me more often about a year ago.

Colton is sixteen and sometimes the six years difference can feel like thirty. He seems so much more mature than me and has outgrown the days he'd pester me to annoy me. Now he only pesters me when he knows I'll think it's silly.

It wasn't always this way though. That's the thing about siblings—our relationships change as we change. I'm just waiting for the day that Levi becomes more tolerable. Tolerable, in this instance, means *I can stand to be around him.*

"Andie, I love your dress!" my dad exclaims as he walks into the living room. I'm wearing a dress my mom found at the thrift store when she bought my new-to-me boots. It's velvet and navy blue. There's a satin sash around the middle that ties into a big bow in the back.

"Thanks, dad," I reply.

"Aren't bows for little girls?" Levi taunts. My dad gives him a look that instantly makes Levi's face scrunch in humiliation. I bet he wishes he had kept his mouth shut.

"Laura loves bows," Colton adds. And my heart jumps a little bit at the mention of something this mysterious girl likes.

"She does?!" I ask. I'm curious if he'll tell me more. "What else does she like?"

"She likes board games. She seems to like yellow the most, even though she never can quite choose one when I ask what her favorite color is. She also likes black coffee, which I've always found weird," he answers, and when he does, I'm positive there is some kind of sparkle in his hazel eyes.

"We're excited to meet her, son," my dad says. He puts a firm hand on Colton's shoulder and squeezes.

My mom enters the room, the smell of patchouli and brown sugar breezing in behind her. "Let's go Wilson crew!"

We begin to load up in the van when Levi says, "I'll take the back, Andie."

The way he says it makes me wonder if our dad mentioned he needed to do something nice for me. Honestly, I liked sitting in the back all by myself. It kind of felt like a little hidden world tucked back on the bench seat. But I don't want my brother to regret doing something nice for me, so I let Levi get in before me to take the backseat.

"Thanks, Levi," I mutter.

The drive to church is quick and quiet, an abnormal occurrence. When we get out of the van, my mom is smiling pleasantly and holding hands with my dad. I'm sure she's happy she didn't have to lecture us about not bickering or keeping our hands to ourselves.

Pastor Will is waiting to greet us at the top of the church steps. When he gets to me, he shakes my hand and says, "Would you like to do the Scripture reading next week, Miranda? You did such a great job last time."

This time I'm not as flustered, but I also wonder if I'm the only one who noticed that I did absolutely awful for my first Scripture reading. "Thanks for asking, but not next week. In a few months, I may be up for it again. Levi, however, would probably love a chance at it."

My brother has already gone ahead of me, but I watch as his head whips around at the mention of his name to Pastor Will. I smile at him with my eyebrows raised up high.

"Levi! That would be great! I'll catch you after service to give you the verses that will need read next week." Pastor Will smiles from ear to ear at Levi, but Levi isn't returning the same facial expression.

"Um, I…" Levi stutters.

"He'd love to," my mom steps in, putting her hands on both of Levi's arms from behind as she peeks over him.

And that was that. Once mom said it was going to be done, it better get done. It didn't matter if it was schoolwork, chores, or Scripture reading. I smile to myself. Maybe this would be the last time he made fun of my bows.

We scoot into our regular row. I love our church pews. That may be a random thing to love but the cushions are a dark green and etched into the sides are elaborate crosses. The wood is stained a very light color. I've always thought they were pretty. Someone who made them put a lot of hard work and detail into them.

We sing my favorite hymn, *In the Sweet By-and-By*. I always love singing about heaven. There's something about knowing God has this beautiful place for us prepared where we won't be hungry or in pain or have any worries. Worries like my really, very bad haircut which seems so inconsequential while I'm singing about heaven. Inconsequential means *not important or significant.* I know God cares about my hair but while singing I realize He cares about my heart the most. And while I've felt heartbroken about my hair, He's been working to heal my broken heart instead of healing my haircut.

The realization makes me sing the hymn with a little more volume. As I'm singing, I feel my mom looking down at me. I look up at her and she smiles and offers her hand to me. I put my hand in hers and squeeze.

When the service is over, I rush to find Sam. She's wearing a very plain black dress, but she's got a sparkling teal jewel hanging from her neck. Her blonde curls seem especially curly today.

"Sam!" I exclaim, wrapping my arms around her in a hug. "Do you know a Laura that goes to your school? She'd be about sixteen. Well, I think. Colton is bringing her over for supper tonight!"

I watch as Sam wrinkles her nose as she thinks through girls in her school.

"I don't know many of the high schoolers," she answers. "I'm trying to think, though. The name sounds familiar."

"Colton says she likes board games, yellow, and black coffee," I reply.

Recognition sparkles in her green eyes. "Wait! The Laura that works at my mom's coffee shop?!"

My eyes feel like they grow two sizes. Colton never said he worked with her, but he also never said he didn't.

"She works at your mom's coffee shop?!" I exclaim.

"If it's the same Laura you are talking about. She goes to my school, and she works the after-school shifts during the week," Sam explains. "She's super nice. I really like her."

"Well apparently my brother does, too!" I giggle.

I look back over at my family who are all talking to different people in the after-church service mingle. Pastor Will is handing over a piece of paper to Levi. Levi looks like he doesn't know what to say. My dad looks over at me and nods his head towards the door.

"I've got to go," I say to Sam.

"Let me know how supper with Laura goes," Sam says before we hug each other again.

Early that evening, I find myself brushing my hair repeatedly while tugging at my clothes to make sure they aren't wrinkled. I want to make sure I look perfect for Laura.

Levi peeks his head inside my door. "This isn't a date, Andie, and it's not your date."

"I just want to make sure Colton isn't embarrassed by me," I say as I look Levi over. He's wearing athletic shorts and a jersey. His hair looks like it has been styled with sweat. "Did you even shower?"

"I'll shower when I usually do. After supper," he mutters.

I know he's been practicing soccer most of the afternoon outside. I'm sure he smells.

"Just don't sit next to Laura," I grumble. "Your stink will surely scare her away."

He leaves my doorway with a huff.

I slide a headband into my hair. It's pink and glittery. I've decided to wear my favorite pair of jeans and a white T-shirt that has frilly sleeves. White is probably risky. My mom said she was fixing pasta and meatballs. I send up a silent prayer that God keeps my white shirt free of marinara stains.

I hear the front door open and my mom squeal with delight as she greets Laura. I can picture my mom hugging her in my mind. My mom isn't subtle about most things.

"I'm so glad to finally meet you, Laura," I hear my mom say as I head down the hallway to meet Laura myself.

When I turn the corner to finally put a face to this mysterious girl my brother likes, I freeze. My jaw drops and I'm not sure I can feel my legs.

She has short hair like me!

Hers is dark, but it's about the same length. She's styled it in a way that makes it look wavy.

"This must be Andie," she says with a beaming smile of sparkling white teeth. I can't seem to get myself to reply or move. I wish I had the ability to become invisible. I'd worked so hard to make sure I looked perfect and now I was an awkward statue standing in my own foyer. I feel my cheeks grow warm with embarrassment.

"This is her," my brother replies. He walks over to me and gently puts an arm around my shoulders. He slightly shakes me, but I still can't seem to blink. "She's just surprised there is another girl here for family supper. She is always having to put up with us boys."

My mom clears her throat. "Excuse me?"

"Sorry, mom. You don't count. If it makes you feel better, dad doesn't either," Colton jokes.

Laura walks over to me. "It's so nice to meet you, Andie. I've heard so much about you. I just love your hair and your headband is so fun."

I manage to blink several times attempting to reboot my brain so I can form words. "I…I…thanks. I like your hair, too."

To add to the shock I'm already experiencing, I realize I actually mean the words. I love her short hair. It looks so pretty on her.

Dear Jesus,

I think maybe I've been wrong about short hair. Maybe.

I asked Laura about her short hair once I found my words again. She wasn't even forced to have her hair cut. She decided she wanted it short herself! She showed me a picture on her phone of her long hair before she had it cut, and it was beautiful, too. She told me that short hair can be just as fun as long hair. I don't think she was lying. She laughs a lot. Colton kept smiling at her. It's weird to see him like a girl so much.

Maybe it isn't my hair that has made life miserable the last several weeks. Maybe it's been me? That's just a hypothesis, Jesus. I'm not saying it's true, yet.

Your Sonshine Sister,

Andie

Chapter 12

We All Have Insecurities

"And she has short hair!" I shout to my other Sonshine Sisters.

We're all sitting on the floor, legs crossed, in a circle, on Saturday night. The week has flown by, and I am so excited to have all my friends in my room to gush about how lovely Laura is.

"Really?!" Caroline asks. "I've been trying to tell you that your short hair isn't such a bad thing, Andie."

"Her hair is beautiful," I sigh. "She's got dark brown hair, and she wore it in this cool, wavy way. Maybe I can figure out how to do that to my hair?"

"I bet if you asked, she'd tell you," Sam says. "I told you I liked her. She's super nice."

"She really is," I agree. "Colton is completely smitten with her."

"Smitten?" Emma asks.

"Love-sick. Obsessed. Hooked like a fish on a line," I giggle. "Like how Ruby Gillis is with Gilbert Blythe, but Laura actually likes Colton unlike Gilbert liking Ruby!"

Anne of Green Gables references always help Emma. She is a fellow fan of the books. If you don't know who these characters are, let me explain. Gilbert likes Anne Shirley. Anne Shirley says she doesn't like Gilbert, but her friend, Ruby Gillis is boy crazy much like Caroline, and is obsessed with Gilbert. If you are still confused, you need to read the books. They are classics.

Emma laughs. "He must like her a lot then!"

"She stayed and played Twister, too," I add.

"When your older siblings date others it can be really hard though," Sarah finally speaks up. Sarah has older siblings, too. Two sisters and a brother. She's the youngest in her family, just like me.

"What do you mean?" I question.

"Well, when they break up, you don't really see them anymore," she answers.

I hadn't really thought about that. Colton bringing Laura home didn't mean he always would.

They could have a fight or decide they don't like each other anymore. She'd no longer visit because she wouldn't be with Colton.

I shake my head. "Well, I'm just going to hope for the best."

Everyone smiles at me, which makes me think they all think that is the best thing to do right now.

"So, Emma? How's Gus?" Sam asks as she's pulling out her sparkly, teal notebook to start jotting down prayer requests.

"His burps still smell horribly," she answers. "I'm having to give him a probiotic now. There was nothing wrong on his x-ray, so the vet says it could be a simple digestive problem."

Gus seemed to have all kinds of problems. First it was fleas, then he had a cold, and now he is dealing with gross-smelling burps. I shake my head, but add, "We can ask my mom if she has some kind of solution?"

My mom used essential oils on everything. She rubbed peppermint on my stomach anytime I had an ache. Surely there was something that could help Gus, too.

"Oh, that would be wonderful," Emma says, pushing her pink glasses back up her nose. "I've felt so bad for him."

I watch as Sam scribbles down Gus's problems on the prayer request paper. Then she asks, "Caroline? Any prayer requests this week?"

Caroline clears her throat. "Well, as you all know from last week, I'm still really sorry about lying and hurting Andie, but not just Andie, I hurt all of you."

"We've forgiven you," Emma interrupts.

"Yes, we have," I add.

"I know," she says while nodding her head. "I'm trying to work on my desire to be noticed. The girls at school have moved on to the next poor girl, but I still feel really lonely trying to figure out how I fit in."

"I'm there for you," Sarah says, reaching over to pat Caroline's hand.

"Thank you, Sarah," Caroline mutters. "I'm so sorry, again. I abandoned my true friend for fake ones because I thought it would get me something I wanted."

Sarah nods. I hadn't really thought about how Sarah must have felt with Caroline choosing to hang out with seventh graders. I wonder if she had felt lonely or hurt, too? Once again, my hair woes had kept me from caring about what my friends cared about and truly knowing what they were going through.

"But I'd just like prayers for not caring so much about what others think of me," Caroline sighs.

Sam writes down the request in the book.

"I'd like to say mine." I say the words and then take a deep breath through my nose. "I want to care less about my hair. I've been so distracted by my haircut and blamed everything horrible that has happened to me on my hair. Really, it wasn't my hair. I know it hasn't been. It's been me choosing to feel bad for myself."

I look down at my lap, feeling like I was once again, the Sonshine Sister that messed up the most.

"Andie," Emma says as she scooches over closer to me. "It's okay that you've cared about your hair. We all care about something about ourselves. I was so upset when I had to get glasses a couple years ago. I thought they would ruin me. I thought I wasn't pretty anymore. Remember?"

"I'm still trying to adjust to my smile with braces," Sarah adds. "They aren't just uncomfortable. They make me look really different."

"I've cared about my hair, too, but not because it is short but because it is so curly. Sometimes it feels like I've got some sort of poodle on my head," Sam says. "I've had to learn how to love my hair."

We all look at Caroline. She stares back at us.

"Well, if we are honest, I've kind of loved everything about myself until those seventh-grade girls made fun of my nose. Now all I can see is my nose in the mirror," she finally mutters.

"See! We've all cared about different things when it comes to how we look," Emma confirms. "It's okay that you care about your hair, it's just you've kind of cared a little too much."

What she says is true. I do remember when Emma wore glasses for the first time. We all thought they were cool, and that Emma looked more like Emma with glasses than without, but she didn't see it that way. Sarah was currently dealing with new braces at the same time I was dealing with a new haircut, and yet Sarah still decided to try out a new sport. Sam and Caroline also had their own insecurities. Insecurity is just a big word that means *lacking confidence or doubting something about yourself.*

It turns out my Sonshine Sisters all could relate to what I was going through in their own unique ways. The problem was I had handled it poorly. I had let my hair become something that didn't make me become more like Jesus, but less like Him.

"And remember," Sam adds. "We're all made in God's image. Short hair, long hair. Big nose, small nose. Glasses, or no glasses. Braces, or no braces. It doesn't matter if we all look different, it matters that we all know He made us to be like Him. None of us are more beautiful than the other."

We all smile at each other.

"This seems like a group hug moment," I suggest. We all scooch ourselves to the middle of the circle and lean into one another.

"To becoming more like Jesus!" Sam exclaims.

"To becoming more like Jesus!" we all say, echoing her words. And it feels good to lean into my Sonshine Sisters. We all have our different problems but having one another to share them with sure makes things feel a lot better.

There's a gentle knock on my bedroom door before it opens. "Hello, ladies! I've got a plate of cookies for you."

"Please tell me there are no chocolate chips!" Emma cries.

My mom laughs, knowing how much Emma dislikes chocolate chips. "I made sugar cookies."

We all jump up to grab the sweet treat my mom just brought us. There are a lot of murmured, "Thanks, Mrs. Wilson!" through ravenous bites.

"I'll leave you girls to your meeting. Sorry for interrupting," she says as she turns to leave my room.

"Never say sorry for bringing cookies," Sarah laughs. "Okay, where were we?"

Sam picks her glittered notebook back up, looking back through the prayer requests.

"I've got a request," Sarah says between bites. "I'm up for setter on the volleyball team. I'd love the position, but I need a lot more practice."

Sam scribbles Sarah's request down before she says, "That leaves me, I guess. I've been asked to try out for chess club. I'm not sure if I want to or not. It would look good on my record, but I'm not sure I can squeeze it in with everything else. I need clarity on what to do."

Sam is always worried about what is on her school record. It began in third grade. She has been set on an Ivy Leage school from the time she could read, which was much sooner than all of us.

She looks up from her notebook. "I think that's all then. Shall we pray?"

We all bow our heads and I listen as Sam prays about each one of our requests for the week. I nod my head the entire time, making sure I'm fully paying attention to what everyone else is needing help with right now. I have over eight weeks of time to make up for after only caring about my hair.

"Amen," she says, and we all repeat, "Amen!"

Dear Jesus,

I know what I need to do. Not just what I need to do, but what I want to do. Give me strength, peace, and confidence to do so.

Your Sonshine Sister,

Andie

Chapter 13

It's Just Hair

It's Monday afternoon after homeschool co-op. I'm sitting in Mrs. Lucy's chair in her salon. It's been nine weeks since my mom had my hair cut off and I'm due for a trim.

"Are you sure?" Mrs. Lucy asks me.

"Chop it off," I demand, smiling.

"Alright," she says, smiling back.

I hear the scissors open and then my strawberry-blonde hair falls against my cheek as the metal snips into the strands.

Turns out short hair isn't so bad after all.

Meet the Author

Hello there! My name is Shelbey Kendall and while I've had a few bad haircuts in the past, I was never homeschooled. However, I have found myself homeschooling my own children. When searching for books for our home library I realized how few books were out there that featured homeschooled children as the main characters. Especially books that address modern dilemmas in current times with characters that feel real, and by real, I mean flawed. A good story has a character you can relate to, whether they make the best choices or not. None of us are perfect, which is why a big part of this new book series is about *becoming more like Jesus!*

As I said, I'm a homeschooling momma. I'm also a wife, homesteader (yes, we have a milk cow and chickens!), and an author. But most importantly, I'm trying to become more like Jesus, too.

I hope this book made you feel seen, taught you something, made you laugh, and inspired you. And the good news is if you have experienced a bad haircut—it grows out! God is kind of awesome about giving us experiences we can grow through!

xoxo,

Shelbey

The Sonshine Sister Club

Book One: Woes of a Really, Very Bad Haircut

Book Two: Do Unto Others

Book Three: Cat Scratch Christmas

Book Four: Secret Admirers and Other Gross Stuff

Book Five: Not All Good Things Are Sweet

Book Six: Yeehaw and Other Farm Stuff

Book Seven: Coming Fall 2024!

Watch for more to come soon in this series!
Follow Andie and her Sonshine Sisters all
through middle school!

Visit

www.thesonshinesisterclub.com

Free coloring sheets and more on the website!

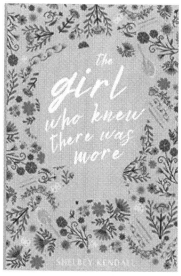

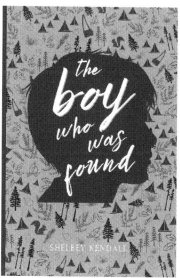

Connect with me!

www.shelbeykendall.com

Instagram: @shelbeykendallauthor

Made in the USA
Coppell, TX
03 September 2024

36726805R00094